The Burdened Duke
William's Story

HISTORICAL REGENCY ROMANCE NOVEL

Dorothy Sheldon

Copyright © 2024 by Dorothy Sheldon
All Rights Reserved.
This book may not be reproduced or transmitted in any form without the written permission of the publisher. In no way is it legal to reproduce, duplicate, or transmit any part of this document in either electronic means or in printed format. Recording of this publication is strictly prohibited and any storage of this document is not allowed unless with written permission from the publisher.

Table of Contents

Chapter One 4
Chapter Two 14
Chapter Three 24
Chapter Four 34
Chapter Five 44
Chapter Six 58
Chapter Seven 66
Chapter Eight 76
Chapter Nine 85
Chapter Ten 93
Chapter Eleven 99
Chapter Twelve 109
Chapter Thirteen 118
Chapter Fourteen 128
Chapter Fifteen 136
Chapter Sixteen 148
Chapter Seventeen 158
Chapter Eighteen 167
Chapter Nineteen 175
Chapter Twenty 181
Chapter Twenty-One 191
Chapter Twenty-Two 200
Chapter Twenty-Three 210
Chapter Twenty-Four 219

Chapter Twenty-Five 225
Epilogue 230
The End 236

Chapter One

July, London

The note had been uncharacteristically enigmatic.

Your Grace,

I have crucial information concerning Our Business. While not as satisfactory as we might have hoped, it certainly represents progress. Allow me to wait upon you at your home in London on the third of this month – which I believe is the day before you depart for Bath – at ten o' clock.

Your Obedient Servant,
Mr. Seeker

William Willenshire, Duke of Dunleigh, glanced at the clock in the corner of the room.

Five past the hour. The wretched man was late. How typical. He fidgeted with his pocket watch, with his cuffs, with his cravat — too tightly tied and digging into his neck — and, of course, with the locket.

It was odd to think that he'd been in possession of the silver necklace for several months now. In that time, all three of his siblings had been married off, one by one, all blissfully happy with their partners, all enjoying their newfound wealth. For such were the stipulations of their late father's will — none of his offspring could lay claim to their inheritance until they were duly wed, and they were afforded but one year to procure a suitable spouse, commencing from the date upon which the will was read.

Frankly, William had not thought they would manage it.

Perhaps I don't know my siblings as well as I thought, he considered grimly. Now that his youngest sibling, Alexander, was recently married, their mother had taken herself off to live with him, her favourite child, and his wife, the quiet and intelligent Abigail. William was all alone in the vast Dunleigh London house, battling unpleasant memories in every room.

It wasn't loneliness, though. Dukes were not allowed to be lonely. William had work to do, not least of all securing *himself* a wife, to fund the estate and title he had inherited as his birthright, regardless of anything else.

He flinched when the door opened, admitting the butler and the stooped figure of Mr. Seeker, the man William had hired to find the owner of the silver locket.

"Mr. Seeker," he said flatly, rising to his feet.

"Apologies for my lateness, your Grace," Mr. Seeker said smoothly. "But I believe my news will console you."

"I suppose I shall find out. Tea, if you please," he added, glancing at the butler. The man bowed and withdrew, leaving William and Mr. Seeker alone. He gestured for the other man to sit and settled himself behind his desk.

"Well, Mr. Seeker? What news do you have?"

Mr. Seeker clasped his fingers together, and William bit back a sigh. He was apparently not going to get a quick answer.

"This case is certainly a strange one and has not produced the quick answer I expected. Let me commend you, your Grace, for being so determined to return this necklace to its owner. It was remarkably chivalrous of you."

William was glad his skin was olive-hued, hiding any blushes. He could remember every instant of the conversation he'd exchanged with the beautiful lady in a dark blue dress, months ago at one of the first balls of the Season. She had been intriguing, bold, and faintly amused at just about everything. She had worn the silver locket around her neck but departed without introducing herself. When William found the locket later, its clasp broken, he had decided to keep it and find the lady himself, rather than simply handing it over to the hostess.

It had been a harder task than he expected. The woman seemed to have... to have melted into thin air. The locket provided a few clues – the initials LB scratched on the back, and a miniature of a child inside. Aside from that, William might have believed that he had imagined her.

"You'll recall my suspicions, your Grace, that the lady in question was one Lavinia Brookford?" Mr. Seeker continued, cutting into William's thoughts.

"I recall, yes."

"Well, I can confirm it. Miss Brookford is the daughter of Lord Brennon, a rather unimportant member of Society. He is a baron, true, but a poor one, and one inclined to bad decisions. He has an interest in breeding horses, it seems, but no knack for selling them on. Miss Brookford is his oldest daughter, and by all accounts has a love for horses herself. I believe the family has recently endured some tragedy or another. To confirm our suspicions, I have it on good authority that Miss Brookford lost a necklace on the date of the party at which you met her. She returned to speak to her hostess and was keen to have the necklace returned to her, although it was not found. Unfortunately, I was unable to procure an address. The family, while in London, have proved remarkably difficult to find. I have heard a rumour that they have returned to their country estate, and I'm sure that with a little time, I will find the address to that place."

"Well done, Mr. Seeker," William managed at last. "You've almost gotten to the bottom of this mystery."

Almost being the operative word. A name really did not mean much. William could attach the name to the sharp, clear face in his mind, but he was no closer than before.

He didn't mention the obvious — that if he had given the necklace to their hostess that night, explaining that he had found it, then Miss Brookford would have been reunited with her locket the very next day, instead of it lying folded in a square of muslin in a drawer.

Mr. Seeker allowed himself a small smile. "Indeed. My advice, your Grace, would be to return the locket by letter, enclosing a brief explanation. Once we have secured the address, of course, which will doubtless happen in a month or two. I am certain the family shall be deeply moved by the lengths to which you have gone."

A month or two. The Season might be all but over then. I'll either be married and rich, or single and thoroughly poor.

Was there a hint of amusement in Mr. Seeker's voice? It certainly was not normal for a man – any man, let alone a duke – to take such pains over returning a necklace to a stranger. Perhaps he ought to feel embarrassment. The feeling made William want to take out the locket again and pass the pad of his thumb over its smooth face. He wasn't entirely sure why the motion was soothing. Should he be ashamed?

William, though, had been trained well enough by his father not to show emotions. Dukes were not permitted to *feel* anything, and the only emotions suitable for a man, apparently, were anger and triumph.

"Perhaps I will, Mr. Seeker, perhaps I will," he responded smoothly, not even blinking. "Perhaps you would prefer to take your tea in the parlour, while I continue my work."

It wasn't really a suggestion, of course. Mr. Seeker did not flinch, to his credit.

"Surely, your Grace," he said, rising to his feet. "I shall keep you updated on my further efforts."

William bit his lip, saying nothing while Mr. Seeker moved towards the door.

"Mr. Seeker?"

The man paused, glancing over his shoulder. William smiled wryly.

"You have done remarkably good work. I am quite in your debt."

Mr. Seeker chuckled. "You have been generous indeed, your Grace. There is no debt to think of. Good day."

He slipped out of the room, closing the door softly behind him, and William was left alone.

He sat still for a moment, tapping his fingers on the wood, then abruptly took out the locket. He set it on the desk and withdrew a sheet of good paper. Already formulating the letter in his head, he picked up a pen, nib hovering above the paper.

Dear Miss Brookford, he would write. *We have not been officially introduced, but I believe I have an item belonging to you...*

He bit his lip. And that would be that. Nothing more to think about. Perhaps they would meet again, perhaps they would not. The Season had reached its pinnacle, and while there were several balls left to attend, it would not be long before members of the *ton* began to leave town, and the Season would dwindle away to nothing over the winter months.

Steady on, man, he scolded himself. *You don't even have her address yet. Perhaps Mr. Seeker won't find it, after all.*

William abruptly replaced his pen, pushing away the blank paper. Instead, he picked up a neat envelope that had been delivered that morning. He recognized the handwriting, and knew it came from his mother. He cracked open the seal and began to read.

Dear William,

I hope your business is proceeding along nicely. Alex, Abigail, and I are having a famous time. She is such a wonderful young woman – I could not wish for a finer daughter-in-law. We are going to Bath at the end of the week, and I believe we shall meet you there, along with Henry and Katherine. London is so tiresome at this point of the Season.

However, I am writing to you on a matter of great importance. It worries me that you are not yet pursuing a courtship. Several suitable young ladies have expressed interest in you, such as Lady Hayward, and even that odd little thing, Miss Bainbridge. Of course, Lady Hayward is far more fashionable, but not <u>quite</u> as rich as Miss Bainbridge. I believe that your father would have been pleased to see you make a match with Miss Bainbridge. He talked often of her family in years gone by, and I think that if he had been alive, he would have arranged it himself.

Still, you have always made it abundantly clear that you will make your own decisions, and so I shall not influence you in any way, other than to remind you that you <u>must</u> marry. You know this already, of course. You may be a jewel in the crown of the ton this year, but nobody considers a poor duke to be a suitable match.

I have the utmost faith in your capabilities, and of course you may rely upon me and your siblings to help you in any way we can.

After all, if Henry, of all people, can secure a bride after being so convinced he would rather give up his inheritance than be forced to marry, I am sure you can manage rather well. I shall be arranging a ball once you return, in honour of

Alex and Abigail, and it will be held at our home in Bath, at Rosewood House.

With your permission, of course. You should attend and make every effort to secure a suitable bride there.

That is all I can presently conceive.

Fond Regards,
Your Mother, the Dowager Duchess of Dunleigh.

William wondered how many mothers signed their letters *fond regards* when writing to their eldest son.

Quite a few, most likely.

The matter of a bride, however, had bothered William a great deal. He'd rather die than marry Lady Hayward, but Miss Bainbridge seemed to be a decent match. She was composed and insightful, exhibiting a candour that bordered upon the unladylike. She would make a good duchess and was quite clearly angling to become his wife. The Bainbridges were shockingly wealthy and powerful, and well known everywhere, but they did not have any titles yet.

They wanted a title, quite badly.

Miss Bainbridge had been very clear. She did not expect to be wooed or even loved. She had hinted at a nice, simple business arrangement, to be settled at the altar. William found her frankness refreshing. After all, he didn't need love. His mother had loved his father – the sentiments not really returned – and look at where that got *her*. Miserable, weak, and broken, distanced from all of her children except one, a shell of a woman.

No, William did not need love, and he was not searching for it. He needed a wife, for many reasons, and it was becoming clear that he was not going to find one here in London.

With a sudden determination, he sprang to his feet and strode towards the bell-pull in the corner. He hauled on it, and the butler appeared a few moments later.

"Your Grace?"

"I am departing for Bath today," William declared resolutely. "Not on the morrow. Are my belongings properly packed?"

The butler blinked. William did not have a reputation as being impulsive. He never did anything unexpected, not without a very good reason.

"Almost, I believe, your Grace."

"Excellent. I would like to leave within the hour. Send word to Rosewood House to let them know to expect me, and have my carriage prepared."

The butler recovered. "At once, your Grace."

He bowed and left the room, leaving William standing by the window, restless for some reason he could not put his finger on. He reached out and took the muslin-wrapped locket and slid it into his pocket.

Chapter Two

There was a hint of rain in the air, unusual for July. Some drops came on Lavinia's cheeks as she hurtled through the forest, hunched over the neck of her horse.

Stepper was a fantastic beast, an almost blood-red stallion with a thick mane of blond-gold hair, seventeen hands high if he was an inch, and frankly the fastest beast Lavinia had ever ridden.

And, more to the point, he was *hers*. He was the foal of the first horse she'd been given, a mare called Rosemary, and she had chosen the stud herself. And now, here was Stepper, the two of them having long since outdistanced the groom who was meant to be accompanying her.

The two of them abruptly burst out of the forest, coming to a gradual stop at the top of a steep, treeless hill, its rocky slope overlooking the house and grounds below.

Panting for breath, Lavinia sat up in the saddle, combing back long red hair from her sweaty neck. It had come undone from the hasty plait she'd tangled it into that morning, hanging down to the middle of her back. The sun was shining again, regardless of the hint of rain, and her skin was entirely too pale to withstand the sunshine for long.

From her vantage point, the Brennon estate looked luxurious and beautiful. One couldn't see the missing roof tiles and overgrown garden from here, on account of them having to dismiss most of the gardeners. She couldn't even see the tiny outbuilding where she and her younger sister, Gillian, had hidden from debt collectors for close to two hours.

Shivering, Lavinia felt the joy from her ride begin to fade away. Their finances were so bad that they had only half participated in the Season, bouncing from place to place instead of having a proper residence, staying with friends and hiring lodgings. The humiliation was intense. It was meant to be Gillian's first Season, and they had to count their pennies. It was awful.

Abruptly, Lavinia turned Stepper's head away from the view and began heading back into the forest. It was almost time for breakfast, and her mother would not be pleased if she was late.

Again.

***

"You are late, Lavinia," Lady Brennon said peevishly, glowering at her oldest daughter over the rim of her teacup. "*Again.*"

"My apologies, Mama," Lavinia answered brusquely, throwing herself into her usual seat. "Lord, I'm famished."

"Oh, for heaven's sake. Could you be a *little* more ladylike?" Lady Brennon burst out.

"I never say that I am hungry," Gillian chipped in smugly. "I always say that I'm not hungry, even if I am. It is much daintier and more ladylike, don't you think, Lavvy?"

"Is it ladylike to starve to death?" Lavinia wondered aloud.

"Probably," Gillian shot back. "Also, you smell badly of horse."

"Oh, that is enough," Lady Brennon sighed, waving her hand. "I relinquish all hope for my daughters. Owen, do convey your sentiments to them."

Lord Brennon, a short, good-natured man with a happy, round face, put down his newspaper and pulled a face at Lavinia.

"Pray, leave the young ladies be, Faye. They may find solace and enjoyment in the tranquility of the countryside, may they not?"

"Pray do not remind me," Lady Brennon replied with a sharpness in her tone. "It vexes me greatly that we are forced to seclude ourselves in this remote location, whilst the season unfolds in London and suitable matches are to be had."

Lord Brennon's smile faded just a little. "I apologise, my darling."

His wife shook her head, lips set in a dissatisfied line. "I know it can't be helped, but still. It's a pity we ran out of friends to stay with."

Lavinia bit her lip, concentrating on filling her plate. For her first Season – this was her third, and it was nearly over – they had stayed in their London townhouse. Shortly after that, their finances tightened again and they were obliged to sell it. Nobody knew, of course, and they often simply rented their old house from the new owners, and pretended it was still theirs.

But the rent was steep, and they could not afford to stay in London for the whole Season. So, Lord Brennon would retreat frequently to their country estate to attend to business, bringing the whole family with him, for a month or two at a time. When they *were* in London, if they wanted to entertain at all while they were there, they were obliged to save up by staying with friends and family. There were ways to live on nothing at all in London, but it required stronger nerves than Lavinia and her family possessed. They were not doing well, not at all.

It was most inconvenient, and Lady Brennon lamented the lack of opportunities it brought. Perhaps it was just because she was then forced to look their situation in the eye and admit that they could no longer afford to even rent the house they had once owned.

Gillian cleared her throat, sitting up a little straighter.

"Do not you worry, Mama, this is the last year we shall have to do this. I intend to make a splendid match, and then you can all come and stay with me every Season. I'll save up my strength and energy, and make sure I do everything I can. Maybe I'll even find Lavvy a half-decent husband."

That brought a smile to everybody's face.

"I certainly hope not," Lavinia remarked tartly, and that even made Gillian laugh a little.

Some of the tension dissolved, although Lavinia was under no illusions that it would stay gone.

A tap on the door heralded the butler, carrying a silver tray in white-gloved hands.

"For your, your Ladyship," he said sombrely, handing it to Lady Brennon. Oddly enough, the lower the family sank, the more determinedly the upper servants clung to their proprieties and traditions. Lavinia knew that they were lucky to have such a faithful household, and that only made her more miserable to think about the inevitable day when they would all have to be dismissed, one by one.

Lady Brennon gulped the last of her tea and took the letter. No, not a letter – Lavinia could see that it was a gilt-edged invitation. Abruptly, the woman gave a squawk of delight, causing her husband to spill his coffee.

"You will never guess who this is from," Lady Brennon crowed, beaming around the table and pressing the invitation to her chest.

"Is it from Lord Tuppers?" Gillian asked hopefully.

"What? That simpleton? No, of course not. It is from the *Dowager Duchess of Dunleigh*. She invites us to a ball at their Bath home, in two weeks' time! That is the famous Rosewood House! Can you believe it?"

Lavinia set her cup down with a click. "We aren't acquainted with the Willenshires, Mama."

Not officially, at least. She had met the new duke once, in a meeting that Lavinia still cringed over. She had had a headache, and felt sick and miserable, longing to be anywhere but that overheated ballroom. As a consequence, she'd found herself out on the balcony with the young duke, and had spoken entirely without propriety, even without thought. No doubt he'd been amused and disgusted all at once, and she ought to consider herself lucky he hadn't thought to ruin her.

Besides, that was the fateful evening when she'd lost Hugh's precious locket. Tears pricked at her eyes at the thought, and she furiously blinked them back. The necklace was gone, and that was that. She was careless. She'd lost it. The last bit of Hugh was lost.

"I met the duchess briefly at Lady Clarissa's ball," Lady Brennon said dismissively. "The dowager duchess, I should say. Can you believe it, Owen? They've invited us – the Willenshires never invited us to anything before – and their Bath residence, no less! Oh, we ought to go."

Lord Brennon bit his lip. "I thought we were staying here a few more weeks."

"Yes, but only think of the benefits," Lady Brennon answered eagerly, leaning across the table to take his hand. "There is a postscript here – the Dowager has invited us to *stay!* I could never have hoped for such a thing! She adds that my company was most refreshing, and that she would enjoy seeing me again, along with my two daughters! Think of what it could be like for Gillian! The opportunities she might have! The Dowager Duchess' balls are always full of eligible gentlemen, everyone is aware of that."

Everybody *did* know that. Everybody wanted an invitation to a Willenshire ball, and not everybody got one. Lavinia glanced sideways at her sister, whose face was taut and pensive.

She's too young for this.

Gillian was nineteen, having already had her come-out delayed by a year. She was remarkably beautiful, with a grace and a sort of sweetness about her that Lavinia had never possessed.

Of the two of us, she resembles Hugh the most, Lavinia thought, and the idea sent a pang through her. She thought, as she often did, of the young, idealized version of Hugh – the sweet, fair-haired boy who had led his sisters through the gardens, creating exciting, imaginative games. That was why she'd chosen the miniature of him as a child to put in her locket, so that she could remember him when they were young and happy and everything was rosy and perfect.

It was childish, perhaps, but the locket was, after all, only for her. Automatically, Lavinia's hand crept up to her neck, where the cool silver of the locket should rest against her collar.

It wasn't there, of course, and she felt the familiar lurch of loss.

How could I have lost it? After all this time, how could I?

It was plain that their mother was pinning all of their hopes on Gillian. Lavinia was too blunt and headstrong to secure a desirable match – if the scandal sheets were to be believed – and besides, at nearly three and twenty, she was too old.

So, if either of the girls were to secure a rich man and save her family, it was going to have to be Gillian. Sweet, beautiful Gillian, whose hair was a much more respectable shade of honey-gold beside Lavinia's vibrant red, with clear blue eyes set in a heart-shaped face, as opposed to her older sister's boring hazel ones. Gillian was kind, biddable, good at the pianoforte, and generally keen to please.

Indeed, she was the one with great prospects before her. Assuming, of course, they could find a way to introduce her to those prospects.

Lord Brennon glanced thoughtfully at his youngest child. It was the manner in which he would appraise a particularly promising gentleman, noting her commendable attributes, her exquisite beauty, and the manner in which she would captivate a prospective purchaser.

It turned Lavinia's stomach to see her father looking at Gillian like that.

Abruptly, she got up.

"I am not particularly hungry," she announced. "I shall go and check on Stepper in the stables. Let me know what you decide."

Without waiting for a response, she turned on her heel and hurried away.

***

"Have you calmed down a little?"

Lavinia, standing in Stepper's stable with a horse brush in each hand, glanced over her shoulder at her sister.

"Who said I was not calm?"

Gillian rolled her eyes. Standing in the entranceway to the stables, the light from outside silhouetted her figure, making her look like a Greek goddess. She was determinedly out of place in a stable.

"I am not a fool, Lavvy. We're going, by the way. We shall be departing; I must inform you. We are bound for Bath, as the Dowager Duchess has graciously extended her invitation for us all to sojourn at her estate, and you are, of course, included in this."

"How lucky I seem to be," Lavinia muttered, brushing Stepper's already glossy coat.

She hoped Gillian would take the hint, but no. After a moment's pause, she heard the crunch of footsteps on old straw and glanced over to see Gillian picking her way towards her.

"Something has upset you, sister. Tell me what it is."

Lavinia closed her eyes. "I don't like the idea of you being sold like a prize mare."

Gillian sighed. "That is simply the way the world is. They don't call the Season a *marriage mart* for nothing, you know. Besides, I would like very much to get married."

Lavinia paused, glancing at her sister. "Do you really?"

"Of course I do. Ladies do want to get married, don't they?"

She snorted. "Not I."

"Oh, no, I forgot that *you* are far too serious and special to *engage in matrimony*."

"Do not be unkind."

Gillian paused, nibbling her lower lip. "I didn't mean to be unkind. I just... it never seemed as though you cared about marriage."

"I do not," Lavinia retorted, continuing to brush Stepper. "Who would want to attach themselves to some fool of a gentleman forever, on the shortest of acquaintances, only to avoid the so-called embarrassment of becoming a spinster? No, thank you. My life is not a display for gentlemen to gawk at and decide whether they wish to marry me or not. I am entirely happy with who I am and the life I lead now. Many women do not have loving parents as we do, and I intend to count my blessings."

Gillian sighed. "If that is how you feel, Lavvy, I shan't contradict you. But I desire to enter into matrimony. I yearn for my own family and to be blessed with children. There is no impropriety in such aspirations, is there?

"I suppose not."

"How gracious of you. I came here just to… to check that you are not going to ruin anything for me at Rosewood House. Could you please come out from there, Lavinia, so we can talk properly?"

Lavinia flinched at that. She could feel her sister's eyes boring into her. Carefully, she set down the horse brushes, gave Stepper one last pat, and emerged from the stall. Stepper's large, liquid brown eyes followed her, mildly curious.

Gillian had found herself a seat on an upturned barrel, and was sitting bolt upright, just as genteel and collected as if she were reclining on a plush velvet stool in one of the finest houses in the land.

"What do you mean by that, Gillian?" Lavinia asked quietly.

Gillian flushed. "I mean that the Season is nearly ending. The Willenshires have gone to Bath, and it will not be long until other grand families follow. Nobody wants to spend winter in London, after all. Time is running out for me. I know quite well that we cannot afford another Season, so I must secure a suitable husband soon. But sometimes you can be… oh, don't be offended, Lavinia, but sometimes you are entirely too blunt. It discourages others, and they are aware that they cannot invite me to a gathering without your presence. I just... I just want you to promise you'll be on your best behaviour. Pray, do not be too disconcerting. Allow me to... to endeavour in seeking a suitable husband, for it shall contribute to our collective contentment."

Lavinia swallowed hard. "I never intended to embarrass you, Gillian."

In a flash. Gillian was on her feet, arms wrapped around her sister.

"You do not embarrass me, Lavvy! I love you with all my heart, you know that. I just need this trip to Bath to be perfect. You understand that, don't you?"

Lavinia pulled back, forcing a wobbly smile. "Of course I understand. Now, shall we talk about which of your dresses we can turn into something a little more fashionable?"

Gillian's face lit up. "Oh, yes, let us do that!"

Chapter Three

Ten Days Later

Rosewood House had always been Mary Willenshire's domain. The Dowager Duchess, everybody knew, had exercised very little authority. She had no control over her children, from whom her husband had distanced her very neatly, and certainly none over her husband.

William had not been thrilled at the prospect of a house party at Rosewood House, but it made Mary happy, and he was not going to be the one to let her down. It was a rare thing to see his mother so happy.

The house was full of excitement, and *people*. When William stepped into the drawing room that evening, intending to read quietly before the fire, he found the room full of his siblings.

It said something about Katherine, Alexander, and Henry that the three of them could make a room feel *full* regardless of its size.

"There he is!" Katherine laughed, stretched out on an armchair before the fire, feet propped up on a footstool. Her husband, the studious Timothy, sat beside her, their hands entangled.

Henry and Eleanor, both always submerged in running their china business, were bent over a pile of papers and sketches on the table, and barely glanced up at him. Alexander was bouncing about the room, doing something to make his siblings laugh, and his quiet wife, Abigail, watched him with fond amusement.

"Good evening to you all," William said, smiling warmly at each of them. Why did it feel so odd to be with his family again? Perhaps it was because they were all paired off, deeply in love, newly rich, and entirely content with their lives.

And he was... well. He was himself. He was none of those things.

"Welcome William! Would you like some tea?" his mother said, leaning forward to pour him a cup. "I'm so glad we were able to go ahead with our usual house gathering this year. It didn't feel right last year, not with your dear father so newly gone."

There was a taut silence, and the siblings glanced at each other.

The late Duke of Dunleigh, father to William, Henry, Katherine, and Alexander, was not mourned at all by his children. He had been a vicious man with exacting standards, and William, as his heir, had borne the brunt of his 'training'. Not one of them had escaped unscathed though.

It was as if the air had gotten thicker. William cleared his throat.

"Well, we're having it this year."

"I've invited a great many new people," Mary continued, oblivious to the atmosphere. "There was a charming woman I met at Lady Clarissa's party, with the most delightful daughter. You might meet her, William. The daughter, I mean. She's nineteen, but this is her first year out. Remarkably pretty, and so sweet. I shall introduce you. I can't quite recall her name. G-something, I believe."

"Thank you, Mother," William responded, taking a gulp of his tea, even though it was still scalding. "Anyone else I should know about?"

"Yes, actually," Mary glanced uneasily around. "I invited Miss Bainbridge and her parents."

William bit the inside of his cheek. "Oh?"

"Yes, they'll arrive with the rest of the guests in three days or so."

"She's made quite a determined set at you, Will," Katherine observed, eyeing her brother intently. "You could do worse."

William smiled tightly. "I'm sure I could. Excuse me for just a moment, I'm going to step out onto the balcony. I need some air."

Nobody objected, and as he turned his back on the happy party, he heard laughter break out at something Alexander had said or done.

William shouldered open the double doors at the opposite end of the drawing room and stepped out onto the small balcony. The air was cool, which was surprising for July, and he breathed it in deeply. The sky was clear, and stars were peeping out one by one over the ridged roofs and whitewashed walls of Bath. It was as if the whole city had been preparing especially for the moonlight, to glow and shine.

He had been there only for a few minutes when he heard a footstep behind him.

"What is it, Kat?" he asked, not turning around.

His sister chuckled, coming to rest her elbows on the wall beside him. "How did you know it was me?"

William shrugged. "Process of elimination. Henry is too engrossed in his work, Alexander is not speaking to me, Mother isn't likely to notice, and it's not as if any of my in-laws would notice anything was amiss."

Katherine pursed her lips. "Why is Alexander not speaking to you?"

William pushed a hand through his hair, the dark chestnut locks all of the Willenshire siblings had, with matching olive skin and hazel eyes. William's eyes, however, were shaped more like his father's. Another similarity he would rather do without.

"Oh, it is not so dire as all that. We did manage a modicum of reconciliation prior to his nuptials, but... alas, it was merely between him and myself after Henry and you departed. And Mother, of course, though she naturally exacerbated the situation. Words were exchanged—words which apologies cannot entirely mitigate."

Katherine frowned. "What sort of words?"

"I'm sure you can imagine. I was not particularly helpful when Alexander was endeavouring to curb his intemperance, and, of course, he was infatuated with Abigail and not in full possession of his faculties. I was rather unkind and unforgiving, I believe. And he said... he said I was just like *him*."

He heard Katherine suck in a breath. No need to explain who *he* was.

"You are nothing like Father," she said stoutly. "I can promise you that."

William smiled thinly. "What if I am, though?"

"You *are not*."

"Do you know what it is to feel like a stranger within the very bounds of your own family?

"Yes," she answered immediately. "I do. Do you not remember? Father thought that ladies ought to be educated separately and kept apart from the men. From the age of thirteen to about seventeen, I exclusively spent my days with Mother. I barely saw you all. It was awful."

"I forgot about that."

"I never can," she muttered. "You aren't like him, William. You aren't cruel enough."

"He can't have started off that way, though. Can he?"

Katherine was silent for a moment. In the end, William broke the silence first.

"I kept the horse, you know."

She blinked at him. "Horse?"

"The horse that killed him."

There was more silence.

"Oh," Katherine managed at last.

William stared out at the star-studded sky, half speaking to himself.

"I'm sure you remember that day. Father wanted me to ride an unbroken horse and threw insults at me when I wouldn't do it. He denounced me as a craven, a weakling, the disgrace of his existence, and so forth. He proclaimed that I was no true gentleman. He brought all of you out to witness my humiliation and climbed on the horse himself to make a point."

"I remember," Katherine said, voice hushed. "The horse threw him. It was a dangerous creature, and you knew it."

"I didn't know it. The thing is, Katherine, I truly was just afraid of the creature. I haven't ridden since."

She reached out and took his hand. "You have nothing to be ashamed of. And I'm glad you kept the horse – it wasn't the horse's fault. I imagine Father spent a good deal of time kicking it and whipping it, trying to get it to behave the way he thought it should. I'm surprised the creature didn't try to attack him before."

There was a short, comfortable silence between them. William felt some of his anxiety draining away.

Some, not all.

"You really don't think I'm like him?" he said, after a pause.

Katherine squeezed his hand. "No, I don't. And deep down, neither does Alex."

"I think... I believe Mother perceives me as a reflection of him. She has expressed this belief on more than one occasion. It is perhaps the reason for her disdain towards me, despite her fervent affection for Father. She foresees what I am destined to become."

Katherine grabbed his shoulders, turning him to face her.

"Stop this, Will. Stop it right now. I won't watch you slip into melancholy, thinking that your future is all preordained for you. It is not. You are your own man. Perhaps we all have some of Father's traits, but it is up to us to become our own people and make our own choices. If we choose to be cruel, or cold, or miserly, then we only have ourselves to blame. Do you hear me?"

"I hear you," William said, smiling wryly.

"Excellent. Now, let us discuss the soiree at the house. I, for one, am quite elated."

"I lament that I cannot share in such delight."

Katherine shot him a sideways glance. "You'll see Miss Bainbridge. I saw something of her in London while you were away, you know. I quite like her, I think. She'd make a fine duchess. She doesn't worry herself with love or courtship, she only thinks of logic and good decisions. I think she would suit you."

"She thinks so, too," William remarked, and Katherine's eyes widened.

"She *spoke* to you about it?"

"Not in so many words. She's very forward, Kat."

"That's a good thing, don't you think?"

"Perhaps. I like ladies to be forthright, but unfortunately, Society does not feel the same."

There was a short pause after that. William shifted his weight, trying not to think of the owner of the locket. That woman had preyed on his mind for longer than she should. Even now, he held the locket in his pocket, its smooth, oval surface gradually warming beneath his fingers. He knew he should return it. And yet, he kept it.

Her face popped into his mind. How had he managed to recall her in such detail? They'd exchanged only one conversation, and on a dark balcony too. She *couldn't* be a very genteel lady, to chat with a man under such circumstances, so freely.

And yet, and yet.

Stop it, he warned himself. *She's not suitable for you. Stop thinking about it. She won't think about you, I guarantee it.*

"Well, it's up to you," Katherine said with finality, cutting into his thoughts. "I like Miss Bainbridge. For what it's worth, she's exactly the sort of girl Papa would approve of, not that that is much of a recommendation. I think she'd suit you, and perhaps you'll fall in love after you are married."

"Is that what you did?" William asked, lifting an eyebrow. "Fell in love after you were married?"

Katherine blushed, and William bit back a smile.

The terms of their father's will had been particularly cruel to Katherine. He had always made it clear that she was not what he wanted his daughter to be and had exerted almost as much effort to break her as he had William. Katherine, however, had a strong character, and had not bent to his will by the time the late Duke met his accident.

Not like me, William thought, with a flush of shame. *I gave in early on.*

Katherine was subject to the same requirements as her brother – to marry within a year or live as a pauper forever.

However, there was an extra stipulation in her case. She had to marry *first*, and if she did not marry, none of her brothers could receive their inheritance.

With the weight of not just her future, but that of her three brothers weighing on her shoulders, Katherine had attacked the marriage mart with desperation, keen to find a match.

She hadn't looked for love, but she had found it. Timothy was their childhood friend, at one time inseparable from William, and wrote popular novels under a pseudonym. He still did, as far as William knew, despite their newfound wealth. He had loved her for years, in secret, and the two of them were perfectly matched.

In fact, all of William's siblings had found their perfect matches. Henry had found a woman to match his intellect and ambition, while Alexander had found a practical, kind young woman who could temper his excesses and help him to become a better man. All of them were in love, and William heartily approved of all of their matches.

His own match, however, was somewhat lacking.

"Falling in love isn't important to me," he said aloud, gaze fixed out on the horizon. "I think Miss Bainbridge will be the best choice for me. She has no expectations of me, and I believe we will enhance each other's lives to a reasonable degree."

"Well, that's a very logical way of looking at it," Katherine said, sounding vaguely disappointed. "Are you going to ask her during the party?"

William bit his lip. "I don't know. Perhaps. I suppose I shall see how the days develop. This will be a good opportunity for us to spend time together and decide whether or not we are well suited."

"The stuff novels are made of," Katherine commented, smiling wryly. "I wish you could fall in love with someone, brother."

"It is not practical. I cannot afford not to marry. And I do mean that in the literal sense, Kat. This estate will sink if I cannot put some money into it, and of course I cannot get to my money until I walk down the aisle."

She huffed. "Father tied us up neatly, did he not?"

There was another short silence, until William spoke again, a trifle uncertainly.

"Did... did you receive a letter from Father on your wedding day? Brought by the solicitor, written when he wrote up the will?"

Katherine clenched her jaw. "I did."

"What did it say? If... if you don't mind telling me, of course."

Katherine sighed, shaking her head. "It was... it was odd. Almost fond. *Almost*. He said that he had always thought that Timothy would be a good match for me, and that shook me somewhat. How could a man I despised all of my life have known me quite so well? It was the sort of letter I could imagine him writing. Henry and Alexander got one, naturally. I believe he told Alex that he was a disappointment."

"That sounds like Father," William grunted. Behind them, the sound of pianoforte music drifted out into the night. He glanced over his shoulder, and saw that Alexander and Abigail were playing a duet. They were laughing, pushing at each other's shoulders, playing wrong notes and giggling.

Something throbbed in William's chest, something decidedly resembling jealousy. He resolutely turned his gaze away.

That kind of life is not for you, he reminded himself. *Dukes do not marry to please themselves.*

"Oh, I almost forgot," Katherine said, jerking him out of his thoughts. "What in the world happened to that silver locket you found, at Lady Clarissa's party? It was months ago, I know, but you were so very taken with it. Did you keep it?"

William bridled. "I did not *keep it*. I have been trying to return it to its rightful owner."

Katherine shot him a quick, intent glance. "Did you find its owner?"

He pointedly did not meet her eye. He was tempted to tell his sister to mind her own business, but that would be quite rude. Besides, then she would *know* that he had something to hide. The necklace seemed to weigh heavy in his pocket, accusing him.

"I did," he answered carelessly. "Apparently, she did try to find her locket, so I daresay she'll be glad to have it returned."

"Ah, well done. Are you going to send it to her, then?"

"I shall return it to her as soon as I can."

And then this will all be over. She'll be glad to get the locket back, and will think no more of the strange duke who kept it for all those months instead of simply giving it to a lady-friend. The duke who tracked her down like a man deranged, the duke who is turning into to a cold, cruel madman just like his father.

William cleared his throat, straightening up from where he rested his elbows on the wall.

"I suppose we ought to go back in. I think I'll have another cup of that tea."

Carefully avoiding his sister's incisive gaze, he turned and hurried inside.

Chapter Four

"We're almost there. We're almost there!"

"Oh, dear! Gillian, have a care! Don't bounce up and down so. You're crushing my gown."

Lavinia pressed herself a little tighter against the side of the carriage, trying to ignore the bickering of her mother and sister.

Their carriage was an old one, built to smaller proportions than its modern equivalents. While *technically* suitable for four, it was a tight squeeze inside, made tighter by the countless bandboxes and bags Lady Brennon and Gillian had insisted upon bringing. It was a landau, more suited to summer-time pleasure drives, but their finances indicated that they use it all the time and pretend it was out of preference.

They were dressed in their best clothes, of course, which meant discomfort and voluminous skirts to manage. One had to make a good impression, after all.

Lavinia sat alongside her father, who was notably silent, lost in his newspaper. She supposed that he would spend most of their stay trying to be invisible, locked away in libraries and in card-rooms, or eating quietly at the dinner table.

She wished she could similarly go unnoticed, though of course not into the card-rooms.

They had passed vast, green fields, all part of the extensive Willenshire estate, and several fields were full of beautiful horses, which Lavinia craned her neck to see as they went by.

I bet I won't get a chance to ride during our stay here. The gentlemen will ride, I daresay, and the ladies will have to resign themselves to walks.

"Do we know whether the Duke will be here this week?" Lavinia found herself saying.

She earned herself an odd look from her mother. "I should think so. It is his house."

"I thought it belonged to the dowager."

"No, of course not. He is the duke, so it is his property. The Dowager has not said anything, but it's fair to assume he will be present. I intend to introduce Gillian to him – rumour has it the Duke is looking for a wife this Season."

Lavinia glanced over at her sister, who smiled weakly at her. Some of her excitement had drained away, perhaps at the reminder that this week was not a holiday, but a serious excursion for her to collect a suitable husband. Lavinia wished she was close enough to take her sister's hand and squeeze it.

The carriage took a turn, and began to climb up a steep, gravelled drive, winding through exquisite gardens. Their path led up towards a large, sprawling building in the Grecian style, with white stone and tall, thick pillars.

They were not the first guests to arrive, of course. Several carriages in varying styles and levels of fashion stood around on the paved courtyard in front of the house, with footmen, valets, and ladies' maids darting to and fro, unloading bags and boxes and trunks.

As the carriage slowed to a halt, they passed an exquisitely dressed trio, an older man and woman and a dark-haired young woman with spectacles. The bespectacled woman eyed them curiously as they went by.

Lady Brennon let out a most unladylike curse, earning a shocked stare from her family.

"That's Miss Bainbridge," she said sourly, folding her arms tight across her chest. "One of the richest women in England, and a conniving little miss into the bargain. She's making a play for the Duke, I just know it."

Gillian sank back into her seat, looking worried.

"She's not as pretty as Gillian," Lavinia spoke up, not sure why she was getting involved at all. "And gentlemen don't like clever women, do they? That's what you always say, Mama. Miss Bainbridge looks entirely too clever for the Duke."

Lady Brennon gave a grunt of acknowledgement. Lord Brennon chuckled, shaking his head.

"Careful, Lavinia. That indicates of bitterness."

Lavinia blushed hotly, the curse of all redheads. "I am not *bitter*, Papa. I am realistic."

"As you say, dear, as you say."

The carriage rolled to a halt in front of a set wide marble steps, and serious-faced footmen in immaculate livery hurried forward to open the doors.

Lavinia was the first one out, to give Gillian time to rearrange and shake out her skirts before emerging into the light.

And, of course, she was closest to the door.

Shifting her weight from foot to foot, Lavinia waited impatiently for her family to manoeuvre themselves out of the carriage. She noticed that the grand steps were immaculate – not a smudge or streak of dirt or dust clung to the fine marble – and found herself wondering how many unfortunate maids had been set to scrubbing those very steps.

And then at last Gillian came tumbling out of the carriage, red-faced and crumpled despite their best efforts, and there was nothing to do but climb the shining marble steps and greet their host.

Ahead, the Bainbridges were just taking their leave, heading towards the wide, red-carpeted staircase, flanked by a small army of servants which they had no doubt brought themselves.

Lavinia thought uneasily of the servants they had brought – Hannah, who served as a head maid and often helped the girls and Lady Brennon dress, and Thomas, a manservant – and hoped they wouldn't look *too* shabby. Was everybody bringing their own servants?

She recognized the Dowager Duchess at once. She was a thin, hollow-looking woman with lank curls and a sense of having been drained of colour and energy. She wore a rich velvet gown, black of course, trimmed with a profusion of lace, pearls, and silver beads. No doubt her gown cost more than Lavinia's and Gillian's put together, but it had the effect of making her seem thinner and frailer than ever.

Still, the smile on her face was genuine.

"Lady Brennon! What a delight!" she cooed, coming forward, hands outstretched. "And these must be your lovely daughters. I am afraid I was not already acquainted with them, but I look forward to getting to know you all better!"

"These are my daughters, Miss Lavinia Brookford and Miss Gillian Brookford."

They curtsied in tandem. The Dowager smiled benignly at them, gaze skipping over Lavinia and dwelling on Gillian.

"My, what a beauty, Lady Brennon! You must be proud. Her prospects, I should think, are very good."

Lady Brennon said something grateful. Lavinia didn't bother to ask for clarification on which daughter the Dowager meant.

"Go straight on upstairs, girls," the Dowager said, beaming. "You'll be shown to your rooms, and you can settle in directly."

They curtsied again, murmuring thanks, and then Lavinia and Gillian were left to sweep away up the wide staircase, deferential servants passing them with downcast eyes.

How am I going to manage? Lavinia thought bleakly. *I hate this place already.*

A straight-backed housekeeper led them along the carpeted hallways, never once glancing back or addressing them. Gillian followed along after the woman, gaze fixed straight ahead, but Lavinia lingered.

"Where do all these doors go to?" she asked once, calling to the housekeeper. The housekeeper was by this time a good way ahead, faltered, turning back with a vague expression of annoyance.

"Bedchambers, morning rooms, one or two upstairs parlours, and so on, Miss," she answered shortly. "The upstairs rooms are seldom used by guests, beyond their rooms, of course. Generally, the unused rooms are kept locked."

A not-so-subtle hint. Gillian nodded earnestly shooting her sister a look which probably meant *pray, stop the questions*.

Lavinia, of course, was not listening.

Why shouldn't I explore a little? I'll likely never stay in such a fine house again, so I might as well make the most of it.

She was already trailing behind, and it was the work of a moment to slow her steps until she was out of sight entirely. Turning around, Lavinia eyed one door in particular, the one which had attracted her attention almost immediately.

It was a huge doorway, arched, with a heavy wooden door and a sparkling brass knob. There was, amusingly, a door-knocker on the outside, shaped classically, a lion with a knocker in its mouth.

She paused, straining her ears, but could hear nothing from inside.

The guests have only just started arriving, she told herself. *I doubt this room is occupied yet. Perhaps not at all. If it is, I can always say that I got lost. If it's not to be used, well, then, it will be locked, won't it?*

She reached out for the brass doorknob, shivering a little at her own daring.

Just a peek won't hurt.

And then the door abruptly whisked open, leaving Lavinia blinking in the doorway, hand still outstretched for the doorknob.

She found herself staring directly at a nicely folded cravat, sitting atop a yellow waistcoat which stretched across a rather broad chest of a remarkably tall man.

And then Lavinia risked a glance up, and all but wilted.

The man towering over her was the most handsome gentleman she'd ever seen in her life. He was tall, as mentioned, with broad shoulders, a strong chest, and a square-jawed, even-featured face. He had olive skin, thick dark hair, and dazzling green eyes.

He was also rather familiar. Oh, yes. Lavinia had met him before, on the balcony of a party some months ago, when she'd talked with a man under most improper circumstances and talked freely and openly about subjects that ladies were not meant to discuss.

She had assumed that the man – a stranger – would not know her again or remember her. More to the point, that she would not meet him again.

"Your Grace," she gasped, realizing with a rush just who exactly this man was.

Goodness, this will be a longer and more humiliating stay than I imagined.

The Duke of Dunleigh peered down at her, face impassive. Did he recognize her? It was impossible to stay. Either way, Lavinia's heart was thundering.

Was he this handsome last time I met him?

"I believe you have the advantage of me," the Duke said at last, after a few seconds of taut silence.

She cleared her throat. "I am Miss Brookford. Miss Lavinia Brookford. I...we... my sister and I just arrived with our family."

A flicker of recognition passed over his face, hastily muffled.

"Miss Brookford," he said, inclining his head.

There was movement behind him, and Lavinia glanced over his broad shoulder into the room. It was a little sitting room, she could see now, and a young woman sat in a chair by an unlit fire, a maid hovering behind her.

Miss Bainbridge, Lavinia realised with a rush. *Of course, Miss Bainbridge is here to see my humiliation.*

"I... I was just exploring," Lavinia stammered, feeling colour rush to her cheeks. "I wondered what was behind all of these doors, you see."

"I see," the Duke echoed. His expression did not shift. Behind him, Miss Bainbridge smiled unkindly.

"This is a private parlour for myself and my family, as the Duke arranged" she said, a smirk playing across her lips. "Would you like to come in and take a look around?"

Lavinia's face was beet red now. "I…"

She was saved from further humiliation by hurrying footsteps along the hallway.

"Lavvy, where did you go… oh."

Gillian came scuttling around the corner, followed by the housekeeper, and pulled up short at the sight of the duke.

"Your Grace," the housekeeper gasped. "Forgive me, I had not realised that Miss Brookford had fallen behind."

He only shook his head. "It's of no matter. Miss Brookford, do please introduce your sister."

Aware that she was failing in her duties as well as humiliating herself, Lavinia introduced Gillian at once.

The Duke bowed to each of them but made no motion to grasp their hands and bestow a kiss upon them.

Lavinia was thoroughly relieved. She had stripped off her gloves the moment she walked into the house, which perhaps had been a trifle presumptuous.

You are not at home, she reminded herself. *You cannot be informal, fool.*

"I shall take the ladies to their room now," the housekeeper said, "and leave Miss Bainbridge and you to your conversation, your Grace."

Something passed over his face, something tight and pained, but the expression disappeared so quickly that Lavinia was not entirely sure she had really seen it at all.

"No need," he said brusquely. "I am just leaving."

The housekeeper nodded and shot a baleful glare at Lavinia.

"Come, Miss Brookford, Miss Gillian. Shall we?"

***

"Well," Gillian announced, parading around their new room with her hands on her hips. *"Well."*

"It is pretty, is it not?" Lavinia admitted, settling herself on the long, padded window seat. She was still reeling from their meeting with the Duke himself.

Could I possibly have humiliated myself even more? Ugh, I am mortified. Imagine, caught "exploring" in the man's own house. What must he think of me?

"Pretty? Just *pretty*? This is the most beautiful bedchamber I have ever seen. And this is a *guest* room, Lavvy! Look at this carpeting! Look at the silk! And the bed…! Goodness, we won't even notice that we're sharing with each other."

Lavinia smiled to herself.

The bedchamber they were shown to was larger than their parlour back home, dominated by a truly vast four-poster bed, draped in silk and satin and covered with brocaded curtains. The windows were huge, a glinting chandelier full of candles hung from the ceiling, and the carpets were so plush and deep that Lavinia thought she could have comfortably slept on the floor instead of the bed.

Their room overlooked the gardens at the back of the house, and she could see distant fields behind the manicured lawns. It was the perfect landscape for riding. From this angle, one would scarcely believe they were so close to the centre of Bath, with all its bustle and Society.

"We must see the Roman Baths," Gillian said, throwing herself backwards onto the bed and stretching out her arms with a sigh, "and I imagine we shall visit the Pump Room quite a few times. Everybody does in Bath, you know."

"Not everybody. Just rich people, like us."

"You mean *Society*?"

"I suppose one could say that."

Gillian propped herself up on her elbows, sighing. "You don't seem pleased, Lavinia. Do take care to temper your advances with the Duke, if you please. He may not appreciate such forwardness."

Lavinia sniffed. "I do not hold much regard for the Duke's preferences, whether they be favourable or adverse."

"Indeed, you ought to consider them. It is, after all, his dwelling."

"How many houses does a single gentleman require? And why, I ask, should one be so grand in its design? I daresay he has never even ventured into this chamber, for instance."

"Lavinia!" Gillian gasped, sitting upright and blushing. "Why are you imagining the Duke coming into our room?"

"I'm not... oh, it does not matter."

Lavinia shifted to lean against the window. The room, despite its high, wide windows, was cool. She wished she could feel the sun on her skin outside.

Movement in one of the distant paddocks caught her eye. Squinting, Lavinia pressed her forehead against the glass.

There was a horse out there. Just one single horse, galloping round and round in wide circles under the watchful eye of a groom.

It was the most beautiful horse she had ever seen. He – she was sure it was a stallion – was bigger even than Stepper, with a glossy black hide and a long, flowing black mane. Its neck was beautifully arched, and muscles rippled under that smooth coat.

What I wouldn't give to ride that horse. I bet it's the duke's own beast. I daresay he never rides it himself but won't let anyone else touch it. Great men can be so very selfish.

She was jerked out of her reverie and entirely unfounded opinions on the duke by Gillian throwing a cushion at her.

"Stop gawping out of the window," Gillian commanded. "There's going to be a fine dinner and probably dancing this evening, so we should start getting ready."

Chapter Five

Several Hours Previously

William was vaguely aware that it was his duty to go downstairs and greet guests alongside his mother. Frankly, he wasn't sure he could face it at the moment. Besides, Mary loved this sort of formality and having him standing awkwardly at her side would not enhance her enjoyment.

He was striding along the hallway, lost in thought, when he heard his name called. His *Christian* name, no less.

Pausing, William glanced over his shoulder to find none other than Miss Bainbridge standing in a doorway, one hand hovering nervously on the doorknob, staring after him. She flashed a quick smile.

"There you are, your Grace. Have you a moment to spare? There's a matter I'd like to discuss with you."

He blinked. "I... what is the matter, Miss Bainbridge? I'm not sure it would be proper."

"My maid is here," she assured him. "It's not improper."

He wavered for a moment, instincts warning him to retire. But Miss Bainbridge looked... well, *nervous*. That was not like her at all. He bit back a sigh.

"Very well. I can spare five minutes."

Smiling in relief, she gestured for him to follow her, which he did.

The room in question was a decently-sized one, set aside as a private parlour for the more *honoured* guests, which apparently the Bainbridges were. Miss Bainbridge seated herself in an armchair beside the fireplace, the promised maid smothering a yawn behind her seat.

"I want to talk to you about a delicate matter," Miss Bainbridge said at last, indicating for him to sit opposite her.

"Oh?"

"You'll recall that I spoke to you rather *bluntly* about… about future plans. Our future plans, to be precise."

A shiver rolled down his spine. Miss Bainbridge wanted to marry him, that much was clear, but it was odd to encounter a woman *quite* so forthright about what she wanted.

"I remember," he said at last.

She lifted an eyebrow. "And have you thought about it?"

He cleared his throat. "Briefly."

"Mm-hm. The thing is, your Grace, I believe that you and I would be well-suited. You're a sensible man, looking for a suitable wife, and I have a great deal to offer, as have you. Frankly, and I don't mean this in a self-congratulatory way, I don't believe you will find a better Duchess in Society this Season."

He bit the inside of his cheek. "You are a fine woman, Miss Bainbridge," he answered, honestly enough. "But marriage is a serious thing, and not something to be rushed."

She inclined her head. "I agree. However, we both know that you do not have the luxury of taking your time, your Grace."

He flinched as if he'd been slapped, staring at her. "I beg your pardon?"

Miss Bainbridge bit back a sigh. "I must tell you that I know about the terms of your father's will. You must marry within a year or lose your inheritance entirely."

There was a brief silence.

"H-How do you know?" William stammered.

She had the grace to look a little ashamed. "My family knows many things, your Grace. For what it's worth, I believe it is terrible for you to be in such a situation. However, there is no denying that you *are* in this situation, and that time is running out for you."

He sagged back into the chair, pinching the bridge of his nose.

"No sense denying it, is there?" he muttered. "I'm a penniless duke. It is rather amusing, is it not?"

Miss Bainbridge hesitated, making an abortive movement forward, as if planning to lay a hand on his arm but changing her mind at the last moment.

"Railing against the way things are is a waste of time," she said firmly. "A man like you might easily take several Seasons to choose a perfect Duchess, but of course you do not have that luxury. That is why I believe my proposal is the best for you. I wish to be Duchess of Dunleigh, and I know without doubt that I can fulfil the position perfectly. I should like us to come to some sort of agreement, or at least an understanding. And soon."

He raised his eyes. "Are you asking me to marry you, Miss Bainbridge."

She allowed herself a small, wry smile, leaning back in her chair to mimic his position.

"Why, yes, your Grace. I suppose I am."

William was silent for a long moment. He did not love Miss Bainbridge, that was clear, but what did it matter? He would never have the chance to fall in love. There simply wasn't time, and he was not the sort of man who fell in love, in any case.

Almost without thinking, he moved his hand to his pocket to touch the locket that sat there, the locket that was no closer to being returned to his owner.

He whisked his hand away, angry at himself for being so silly.

I must marry. I have duties. Surely Miss Bainbridge, with her logical thinking and cool manners, is the best choice!

"I accept," he heard himself say. "I accept your proposal, Miss Bainbridge."

Her face lit up. "Excellent. There is no need to make an announcement anytime soon. We can wait until after the house party is done, and then Society will believe that we formed an attachment here. Marriages of convenience are the norm, but the *ton* will expect us to pretend it is a love match. It is annoying, but there it is."

He nodded, feeling as if his head were underwater, ears full and head ringing.

"I shall leave the announcement to your discretion," he said at last, rising unsteadily to his feet.

Engaged. I'm engaged. I have just gotten engaged to Miss Victoria Bainbridge.

He stumbled towards the door, suddenly eager to leave the room at once, keen to get out as soon as possible. He yanked open the door, and found himself face to face with a beautiful, surprised-looking young woman.

No, not any young woman.

Miss Lavinia Brookford. The woman he had met at the party a lifetime ago, the owner of the locket he held in his pocket.

Recognition flashed over her face.

"Your Grace," she gasped.

What have I done? William thought, fingers tightening on the doorknob. *What have I done?*

***

Later, That Day, Shortly Before Suppertime

William's head was pounding. He wasn't entirely sure when his headache had arrived, but it was fairly sure it was during his conversation with Miss Bainbridge. William reviewed the conversation he had had with Miss Bainbridge only a few hours ago. He kept thinking of Miss Brookford, too, and hated the way his chest tightened at the thought of her.

I should have reviewed my mother's guest list, then I would have seen her name. I would have known. I would have been prepared. I fear that I have made a rather serious mistake.

Would he have accepted Miss Bainbridge's proposal if he had known he would meet Lavinia Brookford at last?

The plain answer was, quite simply, no.

It was too late for a change of heart, though. He was more or less engaged to Miss Bainbridge. While there was only herself and her maid to witness the exchange, no gentleman would go back on his word in such a matter.

William eyed his reflection impassively. His valet was gone, the man's work done, and the party downstairs was already underway. His mother was in charge of it all, naturally, and dinner would be a truly marvellous event. There would be dancing first, though, to allow people to work up an appetite for the supper.

Or something like that. William did not intend to dance before dinner. Not much, at least. He would be expected to stand up at least once, and the question of *who* he would dance with would be on everybody's lips.

Katherine would be a perfect solution – dancing with one's sister, assuming it wasn't a waltz or anything improper, was a good way to avoid showing attention to any lady in particular – but she had already mentioned that she would not be dancing tonight.

His mother wouldn't be dancing – and if she did, not with him – and so that meant that William would have to choose a partner from among the ladies staying at their house.

Who to choose, though?

Miss Bainbridge was here, of course. She'd greeted him with a cool, disinterested smile and glided off with her family earlier on. There were half a dozen or so other young ladies, all pretty and young and looking for husbands, and even the most obtuse man could have read hope in the looks they shot at him.

As he'd known she would, Miss Lavinia Brookford fought her way to the front of his mind. He would have known that she would be here, naturally if he had reviewed the invitations.

And, of course, it was ideal for returning the necklace.

Aware that he was only postponing the moment he had to go downstairs and join his guests, William wandered over to his wardrobe, opening the drawer that held his various jewels. The little muslin-wrapped parcel lay in the corner, and he carefully unfolded it to reveal the glinting silvery locket.

Miss Brookford's locket.

It would be the easiest thing in the world to return it to her now. He could slip it into his pocket, go downstairs, and find her.

"Here you are, Miss Brookford," he would say, airily handing her the necklace. *"I believe this is yours?"*

She would stare at it, surprised, and then glance up at him.

"Oh! Thank you! I feared I had misplaced this treasured item. Pray, might I inquire how you came by it?"

"Ah, I believe it slipped from your possession and, upon noticing it, I took the liberty of retrieving it with the intention of returning it to you."

"But how, pray tell, did you ascertain that it belonged to me? We have not been introduced, as you rightly noted. Might you not have entrusted it to our host instead? For how long, if I may ask, have you held onto this necklace?"

Of course, he had no answers to those very good and relevant questions.

And then it would be over. The locket returned, he could put Miss Brookford out of his mind and concentrate on the much more pressing matter of his impending marriage.

Assuming, of course, that he could choose a suitable bride.

No.

William set the wrapped necklace back into the drawer, closing it firmly. He would return the locket, of course he would, but not *just* yet. He would see how things stood between Miss Brookford and him, and he would choose his moment. As if he'd forgotten all about the locket until now.

He certainly would not tell her he'd hired a private investigator to discover who the necklace belonged to.

Glancing at the clock on his mantelpiece, William bit back a sigh. No more delays. He would really have to attend the gathering now.

***

The party was in full swing. William did not recognize half of the guests – his mother's friends, no doubt – but they all seemed to know him. He weaved his way through the ballroom, suddenly keen for a deep glass of brandy. Or wine, or whiskey, or just about anything to take the edge off the evening.

There were countless eyes on him, itching at the back of his neck and making him squirm. William hated being looked at, and hated having to pretend that he did not care even more. Ladies and gentlemen alike were eyeing him, no doubt whispering about how serious he seemed, whether he would turn out to be the same sort of tyrant as his father. Who would he marry? Would he marry? Would any woman take the risk? Rich, young, and handsome he was, but his father was all of those things once upon a time.

Oh, yes, William read the scandal sheets diligently. He was aware of what was said about him, and the opinions the world held of his father. Accurate opinions, for the most part, but now they were being applied liberally to him.

He noticed young ladies eyeing him thoughtfully, taking in his well-dressed form and broad shoulders, thick hair and good, even features.

They weren't seeing him, though. They were seeing the dukedom, the fine house, and the money they imagined that awaited them if they engaged into matrimony with the Duke.

It was a relief when a familiar face materialized out of the crowds, heading his way.

"Good evening, brother," Alexander said, grinning. "You look lost."

"I detest soirees."

"Don't we all. Well, I don't, but Abigail is deeply uncomfortable. Come, let us take a walk around the room."

William would have much preferred to find a quiet corner and sit unnoticed, but that was unlikely to happen. Abruptly, Alexander nudged him, nodding.

"Observe, there stands Mother's acquaintance, Lady Brennon or some such appellation. She is a most amiable lady, and it warms my heart to witness Mother cultivating new friendships. Her daughters appear to be of fine character as well. The eldest approached Abigail with the utmost friendliness and engaged her in conversation without hesitation. Abigail seems quite enchanted."

William felt as though his chest were tightening. Glancing over to where Alexander pointed, he saw the three women enter the ballroom.

Lady Brennon walked in front, head held high, wearing a blue gown which hadn't been in fashion for at least three years, although it suited her well. Her two daughters came behind her.

The youngest girl, Miss Gillian, was wearing the newest and prettiest gown. It was a shade of pale lilac – pastels were in this Season, if William was not mistaken – and the ruffled, airy style suited her very well, complimenting her honey-gold hair. Several gentlemen threw her appraising, approving glances as she passed by.

But William's eye was drawn, not to the sweet and beautiful Miss Gillian, but her older sister.

Miss Lavinia Brookford wore a green gown that belonged to last year's styles, sleeves too long and heavy to suit a ballroom. The colour made her red hair glow like fire, so that one barely noticed its simple style. She kept her head up, gaze raking through the ballroom, meeting the eyes of gentlemen and ladies alike squarely.

The music suddenly started up in earnest, making William jump. There was a flurry of excitement, with gentlemen and ladies pairing off and taking their places on the dance floor.

As he watched, a gentleman approached the two Brookford girls, bowing and making his introductions. To William's surprise, he seemed to be asking Miss Gillian to dance, instead of her older sister.

Miss Gillian demurred, glancing up at her sister for instruction. Miss Lavinia gave the tiniest of nods, and Miss Gillian turned back to the man with a shy smile.

He led her off, leaving Miss Lavinia to stand alongside her mother, arms folded. She seemed to recollect that her arms *were* folded, which was not proper for a lady, and unwillingly untangled her arms, letting them hang by her side. She discreetly checked the clock above the mantelpiece, and William bit back a wry smile.

An elbow dug into his ribs, waking him up from his reverie.

"It is impolite to stare," Alexander said pointedly, lifting his eyebrows.

William flushed. "I haven't the faintest idea what you are talking about."

"You most certainly do. Miss Lavinia. You've stared at her like you're seeing a ghost. Are you shocked by her unfashionable gown, or do you admire her?"

"Neither."

"Hmph. Well, are you going to dance? It's the first dance to open the ball, *and* to start off Mother's ball. You ought to dance. Why not ask Miss Lavinia? Mr. Hasselford just asked her younger sister to dance instead of her, which is rather rude in my opinion."

"I'm sure Miss Lavinia is not offended. Mr. Hasselford is a simpleton."

"That's a fair observation. Nevertheless, you ought to make inquiry of her. She has not signified an interest in you, and as she is nearly a spinster, it is likely her ambitions do not extend in your direction. No one will raise an eyebrow should you choose to ask her."

William wavered. Could he ask her? Should he ask her?

And then Alexander hissed between his teeth, nudging him again.

"Wait a moment. Miss Bainbridge is coming our way."

The woman in question slipped quietly through the crowds, small and unobtrusive among the frilly pastel gowns around her. She wore a simple dress in a deep blue, flattering but hardly eye-catching. Miss Bainbridge had an interesting face, round and even featured, with large blue eyes and dark hair dressed in a somewhat austere style, with a pair of round spectacles perched on her nose.

"Your Grace," she said, making a neat curtsey. "It's a pleasure to see you again."

"And you, Miss Bainbridge."

Many ladies took their mammas along with them when it came to approaching gentlemen. The rules for women were much more austere than that for men – the idea of pressing oneself on a gentleman's notice was rather disgusting for ladies, and that involved talking to a man who had not expressed interest in speaking to her first.

It seemed ridiculous to William. He remembered all of these rules from when Katherine was younger, and their father was making a valiant effort to compress his daughter into the social mould for young women. Katherine, naturally, did not fit, despite him applying all of his force.

Most other ladies submitted, and he couldn't particularly blame them. However, Miss Bainbridge struck him as a woman who had politely refused to become the model of a Proper Young Lady, and quietly went on her own way.

Miss Lavinia also seemed like that sort of woman, albeit a little louder about her nonconformity than Miss Bainbridge.

Miss Bainbridge was also much richer, and money meant that people would forgive almost everything.

Alexander greeted Miss Bainbridge, drawing William back to the present.

"My congratulations on your marriage, Lord Willenshire," Miss Bainbridge said, voice cool and even. "Miss Abigail Atwater was an unusual choice."

Alexander visibly bristled. "Unusual? Why, because she has no dowry?"

Miss Bainbridge allowed herself the tiniest of smiles. "I only came to offer congratulations."

"Right. Well, thank you. I shall pass your congratulations on to Abigail."

He made his excuses, shooting a significant look at his older brother, and melted away into the crowd. Miss Bainbridge watched him go, eyes narrowed.

"Your brother appears to be thriving," she remarked, as if seamlessly continuing a discussion from earlier.

"He is," William said, feeling protective for a reason he could not quite identify.

"He has drunk nothing but water and lemonade all night."

Ah. That was what she was getting at. William cleared his throat. "Yes, I believe Alexander avoids alcohol these days. He said he has lost the taste for it."

"I imagine we have Miss Atwater to thank for that? Forgive me, I ought to call her Lady Willenshire, but there are two of them now. You have an extensive family."

William fidgeted. "Yes, I do."

She smiled thinly up at him. If she could sense his discomfort, she did not care. Her round spectacles glinted in the copious candlelight, making it difficult to read the expression in her eyes.

"You are not dancing, your Grace."

"Neither are you."

She laughed at that. "Then I assume you know why I'm here. Tell me, your Grace, have you thought at all about our discussion?"

He cleared his throat, her stare burning into him.

"I... I'm not sure that is something we should discuss."

"Oh, come, your Grace. Being demure does not suit you. I'll be frank in a way you will not benefit from again in this society. Everyone is musing and conversing about your forthcoming nuptials. Every unmarried lady present envisions herself as the Duchess of Dunleigh. You would indeed make an exemplary husband, and every woman perceives it. You could readily have your choice, and all are acutely aware of it. That, sadly, signifies that every action you undertake, every word you utter, is subject to scrutiny. Should you be unduly careless, you may find yourself ensnared by some enterprising young lady, all but coerced into matrimony."

He eyed her for a moment. "I imagine I know what that feels like."

She allowed herself a small smile. "Why not exercise what little agency you have left? Announce your bride, before Society chooses one for you."

He sighed. "Has anyone ever told you, Miss Bainbridge, that you are a terrifying young woman?"

"On several occasions, yes," she answered, without missing a beat. "Now, to business."

"This discussion was *not* business?"

"Certainly not. It was free advice, which I do not usually hand out. No, I see that the dancing is beginning. You'll be expected to dance, your Grace."

"Yes, I know. I have to ask a lady to dance, and I am paralysed by indecision."

Unbidden, his gaze wandered over to where Miss Brookford stood beside her mother. A gentleman was speaking to her now, a man he did not recognize. They were just talking at the moment, but no doubt he'd ask her to dance in a moment.

William's heart sank, and then sank further at the realization that he was *disappointed.*

"Come, your Grace," Miss Bainbridge said, intent gaze landing squarely on William's face. "Ask me to dance, won't you? It's what expected of us both, I believe."

She offered a small smile, wry and meaningful.

She doesn't want to dance either, he thought, the inevitability settling over him like a heavy blanket. *And yet we both have to.*

"Miss Bainbridge," he said, offering his arm with a flourish, "will you dance with me?"

She affected surprise. "Goodness, your Grace, what a surprise! But yes, I shall dance with you."

Arm in arm, they moved towards the dance floor. He did not allow himself to look back at Miss Brookford.

Chapter Six

"Lavvy, I am quite exhausted!" Gillian gasped, flopping down into the seat her sister had procured for her. "I can scarcely stand."

"I can see that," Lavinia said, chuckling. "You've danced every single dance so far. Pray, do take your ease, or we shall be compelled to lift you from the floor shortly."

In fact, Gillian *looked* exhausted. At the beginning of the ball, she had been in excellent looks, but now her skin was pale and waxy. There was a sheen of sweat around her forehead and temples, which she delicately dabbed away with a lace-edged handkerchief. Lavinia eyed her sister worriedly. Gillian needed a drink, perhaps some lemonade or simple ice water, but the second Lavinia turned her back, their mother would likely find another gentleman to ask Gillian to dance.

The fact was that the girls were not used to such intensive dancing. In London, crowded as it was with belles and husband-hungry young ladies, every gentleman had about four ladies wanting to dance with him for every set. Gillian was pretty, and danced a good deal in London, but her dance card was never so full as it was tonight. Besides, it was well past midnight, and the dancing looked set to go on for hours.

"I think Gillian is tired, Mama," Lavinia said, in a low voice.

Lady Brennon tutted. "She can't be tired. The night is still young."

"It is no longer tonight, Mama. It is tomorrow. Let her sit out a few dances to regain her strength."

"When I was your age, I could dance all night without stopping. I used to wear out dancing slippers in no time."

Lavinia sighed. "Yes, Mama, but Gillian isn't used to that. You know she isn't strong. Let her rest."

"Oh, very well, very well! Her next set is empty, anyway."

Lavinia allowed herself to relax a little, flashing a smile at her sister. Gillian smiled gratefully back.

She was breathless, Lavinia noticed. As a child, Gillian had always had a weak chest, and the unforgiving dancing and the stifling heat of the ballroom was certainly not helping.

Suddenly, Lady Brennon perked up. "Ah, here comes the Dowager and the Duke! Sit up straight, Gillian. Hadn't you better stand up?"

"Mama, she's resting!"

"Oh, alright, alright! I was just *saying*. Here they come."

The Dowager appeared, face flushed with the heat and the triumph of a successful party. Her son followed, looking distinctly less enthusiastic.

The Duke was suffering more from the heat, his olive skin dappled with sweat in places. His hair, immaculately styled and pomaded, was beginning to slip free. He pushed back a lock of chestnut hair from his forehead, cool eyes raking over them all, and Lavinia hastily looked away.

"Sitting down already, Miss Gillian?" the Dowager laughed. "Good heavens, do not tell me you are fatigued!"

"My sister is tired, your Grace," Lavinia spoke up, before anyone else could say anything. "She is indulging in a well-deserved respite. I cannot speak for you, your Grace, but I have not partaken in every dance this evening, and thus I can scarcely fathom the extent of her fatigue by this hour.

Those thin dance slippers don't provide much support, I think."

The Dowager barely seemed to be looking at Lavinia, and no doubt did not listen to a word she had said. She was looking at Gillian with a speculative look, and then at her son.

Lavinia's heart sank. Of course, the Dowager was thinking that Gillian would make a pretty bride for her son, and become a nice, malleable Duchess.

She certainly would, but Lavinia was sure that her sister was not particularly drawn to the duke at all, besides admiring his admittedly good looks.

"If you are not dancing with anyone this set," the Dowager said, shooting a pointed look at her son, "perhaps William and you ought to stand up together."

This, Lavinia thought clearly, *is not fair.*

She could see her mother brightening, and no doubt images of Gillian, Duchess of Dunleigh, were flashing before her eyes. The Duke himself glanced at Gillian, sitting breathless and pale on the chair, and his brow flickered. Perhaps he thought she was too tired to dance, but a proper gentleman would not do anything to imply that he did *not* want to dance with a lady.

Already, Lavinia could see Gillian trying to catch her breath, to straighten up in her chair, ready for a dance that she was too tired for. The duke would ask at any moment, and then it would be too late.

Lavinia was speaking before she knew it.

"I quite envy my sister," she said, earning herself a surprised glance from the Dowager – who had doubtless forgotten that she even existed – and a warning stare from her mother. "She has danced every set so far, while I am left to sit alone with the matrons and chaperones."

It was the most pointed thing she could imagine saying, without flatly asking the duke if he would dance with her instead of Gillian.

The duke smiled politely. "Then perhaps you would like to stand up with me for this set, Miss Brookford."

Ignoring her mother's furious glare, Lavinia smiled weakly.

"I should love to, your Grace."

There was no time for anything else, as the music was already starting up. The duke offered her his hand, and she took it, twisting to look back over her shoulder at Gillian. Her sister was sinking back into her seat, blinking tiredly.

The duke walked quickly, obliging her to scurry along at his side, and he kept his gaze fixed on the couples milling around the floor ahead of them. It was, to Lavinia's chagrin, a waltz.

That meant that not only would she have to stand uncomfortably close to the duke, but she would also have to talk to him.

"I hope you don't mind what I said," she blurted out, as they turned to face each other. "My sister is not strong. Mama would have her dance herself to death, I think."

She immediately regretted saying that. It wasn't a kind thing to say about one's mother – even if it was true – and the duke blinked, as if surprised.

The music began, and Lavinia hurriedly grabbed at the duke's shoulder, taking his hand in hers. His free hand landed tentatively on her waist, as the dance required, and she could feel the warmth of his palm seeping through her gown.

Best not to think about it.

"You seem concerned for your sister's health," the duke said, after a moment of dancing. It was not a vigorous dance, and they both had plenty of breath and opportunity to talk. Lavinia concentrated on staring at his shimmering cravat pin, instead of craning her head back to look at his face. "Perhaps she should dance a little less."

"Perhaps you should suggest that to our mother, then. She doesn't listen to *me*."

Another improper and deeply unladylike speech. Lavinia flushed, glancing up at the duke's face to see if he were shocked.

He was only smiling wryly, however.

"You speak your mind, Miss Brookford. I admire that. It's not a quality I possess myself, but I admire it in others."

"I don't admire it in myself. If I were to receive a penny for every instance my tongue has led me into indiscretion, I should be in possession of a considerable fortune at this very moment."

He chuckled at that, and Lavinia shot an amazed glance upwards, to double check that he was, indeed, *laughing*.

"Goodness, your Grace, did I just hear you laugh? And here I thought you were carved from stone."

He laughed again, shaking his head.

"Miss Brookford, you remind me of my youngest brother."

"Lord Alexander Willenshire? I shall take that as a compliment."

"It *is* a compliment."

They whirled round the dance floor, picking up speed. This dance, Lavinia guessed, was going to be short. Dinner had come and gone, but there was to be a small supper spread in the supper room soon enough. It seemed that the Willenshires intended to keep London hours, with an additional meal conducted after midnight and followed by more dancing. After all, when one could sleep until midday and beyond the following day, why not stay up late?

She was aware of glances thrown her way. Most of the looks were not pleased. It occurred to Lavinia, just a little too late, that she was dancing with the most eligible man in London *or* in Bath at this moment, and she herself was a penniless spinster.

What was more, she had made him *laugh*.

He's not going to talk about our unfortunate meeting earlier in the Season, Lavinia realised in a rush. The relief was immense. *He is being a gentleman and pretending it did not happen.*

Or perhaps he's simply forgotten, and I am not as memorable as I would have liked.

That last thought was not particularly pleasant, and she dismissed it at once.

The music ended with a flourish, and the two of them pulled apart.

She found that she missed the warmth of the duke's hand on her waist. Now *that* was a disorienting thought.

The duke's gaze flitted around the room, dwelling on one corner in particular. Lavinia had a feeling that if she looked over, she would see the Bainbridges there.

"May I escort you to the dining room should you wish for a repast? I fear you may be fatigued after such a long and eventful evening," the duke said, in a rush.

The simple answer was no. Lavinia did not like being *escorted* anywhere. She was a grown woman with perfectly good legs, and certainly did not require support to reach the dining room, of all places.

But, of course, the duke would *have* to escort *somebody* in, and he suddenly seemed keen to escort her. As opposed to any number of the eager, grasping young ladies who would make something of the invitation.

"Why, yes," she said, as if there was any other reply. "Thank you, your Grace."

Dozens of gazes fixed on Lavinia's face. The Dowager led the way, of course, on the arm of her youngest and favourite child, Lord Alexander. The duke came next, with his siblings trailing behind him with their respective spouses, and then the rest of the party.

Lavinia was well aware that at least half of the ladies there – and even more of their mammas, she guessed – had coveted her place. With the duke escorting her into the dining room, she would be able to sit beside him and have the opportunity to converse. She wondered whether her mother would ever forgive her for snatching the opportunity from Gillian.

Oh, well.

Lavinia tried to keep her head up and concentrated on not embarrassing herself in some way. Plenty of jealous ladies would be glaring at her, finding fault with her hair, her face, her figure, her way of walking, her *age*, and of course, her lack of money.

She found herself thinking about Miss Bainbridge.

The woman in question was not a Society beauty, but that did not seem to matter in the slightest around a woman like *her*. She was forthright, oozing confidence, with a way about her that made people quiet down and listen. And, of course, she was fabulously wealthy. *She* would never shift uncomfortably on the arm of a duke, longing to duck her head and avoid the stares levelled her way. She would keep her head up, eyes straight ahead, and enjoy the attention as her due.

Some of Lavinia's awkwardness faded away as they filed in the dining room, with people finding their chairs.

"I never asked, Miss Brookford," the duke said, pulling out a chair for her, "do you possess a variety of hobbies and interests? As it appears we shall be seated together and it would be delightful to discover some common ground between us."

She sat, feeling a little more herself again. The duke's sister was seated opposite and flashed her an encouraging smile and a wink.

"I'm afraid my pursuits aren't particularly ladylike," Lavinia said, wincing. "I like to be out of doors as much as possible."

"It's a healthy occupation. I am myself often closeted in my study, and it feels like such a waste of a fine day."

"Oh, I agree. Rainy days are fine to spend inside – I enjoy reading, although nothing properly *improving*, you know – but on fine days, nothing suits me better than taking my horses out for a gallop. Are you fond of horse riding, your Grace?"

It was a simple enough question. It had never occurred to Lavinia that there could be any answer beyond yes.

To her surprise, though, the duke stiffened, the smile dropping from his face like a stone.

"No," he said shortly. "No, I do not. More wine?"

Chapter Seven

He'd been too brusque, that was for certain. William had seen Miss Brookford flinch when he'd rudely informed her that he did not care for horse riding. His change of subject had been clumsy and fooled nobody. Thank heaven only she had heard it, although doubtless she would mention the conversation to others.

He felt eyes on him across the table, and didn't need to look to know that it was Miss Bainbridge. Her expression, no doubt, would be impassive and unreadable as always, but there would be a flash of annoyance in her clear eyes. They had a bargain. Oh, the engagement, such as it was, would not become common knowledge for a while, but that didn't matter.

I am a betrothed man, just about. I should have walked away from her. I should have said no.

Regret, it must be said, was a painful and inescapable thing.

Miss Bainbridge believed that she and William were to marry, sooner rather than later. So did the rest of Society, as a matter of fact, even if they didn't know about the betrothal.

And then he went ahead and waltzed with an obscure spinster and escorted her into dinner.

Yes, this would be talked about a great deal, after tonight. William bit back a sigh. If only his mother hadn't tried to force him to dance with that poor, exhausted girl. Miss Gillian looked tired, and he suspected this hour was much later than she was used to staying up.

And there were hours to go.

He glanced sideways at his companion. Miss Brookford was staring down at her plate, a frown between her brows. He hoped he hadn't offended her *too* much. She didn't strike him as a woman who was easily offended.

"I believe your father has an interest in breeding horses," he heard himself say. It was hard to feign interest in such a subject, but he was rewarded when Miss Brookford's face lit up. "I assume that is where your love of horses came from?"

"Oh, yes! My favourite horse is Stepper, I bred him myself. He's quite remarkable. Only last week, on a gallop across the hills, we..."

She launched into a story about her horse, about its credentials and breeding, speed and strength. William was not interested, of course, but he smiled politely. It was pleasant to see people lit up with interest, visibly happy to talk about their favourite subject. There was something about Miss Brookford, about her unselfconscious chatter, that made him want to keep listening.

She had a pleasant face, too. William was used to seeing pretty women – Society was full of beauties – but Miss Brookford's features were intriguing in a way he had not encountered before.

"... something scared him, I think," Miss Brookford was saying now. "Stepper doesn't scare easily these days, but something darted across the path. A rabbit, perhaps? He reared up, and I had a hard time keeping my seat, I can tell you that."

William's throat tightened. Suddenly, he was plain old Lord William Willenshire again, eldest son to a duke, standing in front of a sweating, mincing beast of a horse, his father's insults ringing in his ears.

"By God, William, you'll mount that horse if it's the last thing you do!"

"I can't, Father. The horse is nervous. It'll throw me."

"Have I raised a coward? Do it at once, or I'll summon your mother and siblings to witness your shame!"

He closed his eyes. The words still stung, despite William knowing, logically, that he was not a coward and the horse had, indeed thrown its rider.

Of course, the rider had been the old Duke, and not William himself.

I would have died. It would have been my neck broken, not Father's. He would be alive, with Henry as his new heir, none of my siblings married, and all of them miserable.

"Y-Your Grace?"

William's eyes snapped open, and he found Miss Brookford watching him, her expression curious and a little concerned.

"Hm?"

"Are you... are you quite well?"

He forced a smile. "Yes, yes, thank you."

She tilted her head to one side, and he had the sense that she was not convinced. To his horror, he felt the urge to blurt it all out – the horse, his father, the *deadline*.

Against all odds, William was saved by his mother.

The dowager rose, smiling shyly at her guests.

"Ladies, shall we retire?"

There was a general kerfuffle of activity, ladies rising to their feet and gentlemen falling over themselves to stand respectfully. William rose too, of course. Miss Brookford eyed her half-finished supper with something like regret, but obediently rose, following the other ladies out of the door.

Miss Bainbridge was one of the last to go, and he felt her eyes lingering on him as she passed. The door closed behind them, and he heard the distant laughter and chatter as the ladies headed away towards the drawing room.

The atmosphere relaxed palpably once the ladies were gone. Jests could grow a little coarser now, men could drink alcohol more freely, and there were fewer sensibilities to offend.

Or so some gentlemen thought.

William shifted uneasily, already dreading the pungent stink of tobacco smoke. Some gentlemen were already lighting up cigars, ordering more brandy.

He flinched when a hand landed on his shoulder and glanced up to see Alexander bending over him.

"Time for billiards, I think," Alexander murmured. "Come. Henry and I are going now, and I do believe Kat is joining us."

"Kat? She hates billiards."

"I do believe she's been playing it with Timothy. *He* is discussing poetry and novels with some chap in the corner, so we can let him alone. You are coming, or are you not?"

William hesitated. A good host should stay with the majority of his guests, but really, he didn't think he could face another few hours talking politely of politics and commerce.

Besides, none of them would notice if he slipped away.

"Surely," he said at last. "I'm coming."

***

"Your turn, Kat."

Katherine grinned unpleasantly, lining up her cue. The billiard balls clicked, bouncing across the green baize, and she managed to pot several at once. The boys groaned aloud.

"You've been practising," Henry said, almost accusingly. "Wait till I get my hands on Timothy. I wager he'll have taught you all sorts of cheating tricks."

"Pray, do not be a curmudgeon, Henry, my dear. Merely because I am besting you all does not imply that I am resorting to foul play."

William chuckled at that, enjoying the surly expressions on his brothers' faces. He wasn't entirely sure how Katherine had managed to slip away from the ladies in the drawing room – they were much more alert than the cigar-and-brandy addled gentlemen in the dining room – but slip away she had. And she was in the company of her brothers so no gossip would arise. They had been playing for about twenty minutes now, and William could feel some of the day's anxiety melting away.

Why couldn't it always be like this between them?

"The Bainbridges aren't pleased with you, Will," Katherine said suddenly, breaking the silence.

William blinked at his sister. "What? Why? What have I done?"

Alexander winced. "You were always so obtuse, Will. No offence."

"You danced the waltz, of all dances, with *Lavinia Brookford*, and then you escorted her into the additional light supper right afterwards," Katherine commented, lifting an eyebrow.

"May I not choose with whom I shall dance, and whom I shall graciously accompany to supper?"

His sister looked at him as if he were a simpleton. "No, of course not. You're the Duke, and their host but you should have chosen somebody else."

"Like Miss Bainbridge," Alexander put in. "They were expecting you to escort her into that additional light supper and were rather offended that it was Miss Brookford."

William felt an uncharacteristic surge of anger. He took his time in responding, lining up his next shot. The billiard balls clicked. He missed.

"And why," he said, as coolly as he could manage, "are the Bainbridges' expectations my responsibility?"

Alexander and Katherine glanced at each other. "Because they believe you're pursuing Miss Bainbridge. You speak to her at every event, she's been invited here, you often dance together, and of course you're a perfect match." Katherine said, speaking slowly. "The Bainbridges aren't penniless little fortune-hunters. They have a great deal of power, and they expect all courtesies. If you aren't pursuing Miss Bainbridge, you ought to make that clear now."

"I didn't say that I wasn't considering her as my duchess," William muttered. "I wasn't aware that Society had us married already."

Lies. It was a lie. Now would be the time to tell his siblings about his agreement with Miss Bainbridge. He willed himself to speak, but it seemed that his lips were sealed closed. Dropping his hand into his pocket, he felt a pang of loss to discover the pocket empty, the silver locket left safely in a drawer on his desk.

Alexander stepped forward to take his turn. "Really, what did you think was going to happen, brother?"

"I for one think that this is shocking," Henry spoke up. He was perched on the window seat, resting his chin on the top of his billiard cue, face black as thunder. "Why should William be forced into matrimony just because she's suitable? I'm sure that Miss Bainbridge is a pleasant young woman, and if William likes her, I'll happily welcome her as my sister-in-law. But it must be *his* choice. His and hers, and no one else's."

"Thank you, Henry. I am glad that *someone* is on my side."

Katherine chuckled. "Perhaps if Henry could get off his high horse and take his turn, the game might progress."

Henry rolled his eyes at that, jumping down from the window seat.

"We have all, indeed, united in matrimony for the sake of love," he remarked, preparing to take his aim. "I never imagined it would come to pass for me, yet here I stand. We three find ourselves exceedingly content, do we not? Why should not William be afforded the same opportunity?

"Because," Alexander said, leaning forward, "the deadline is only a handful of months away, and the Season is winding down. The pinnacle of the Season has come and gone, and we've retreated to Bath. William has to marry this year – and I say he *has* to marry, because he is the one who has the estate to look after. It's vital that he marries, and soon. Miss Bainbridge is a suitable choice."

"I don't like her," Henry announced, straightening up. "She's too conniving for my liking. She knows her worth and the worth of everyone around her and treats them accordingly."

"And is that a flaw?" Katherine shot back. "Clever women are a rarity in our Society."

Before he knew what he was doing, William was speaking.

"Miss Brookford is a clever woman."

His siblings went quiet, glancing at each other and then at him.

"You have a fancy for Miss Brookford, then?" Alexander said carefully. "The older one, not Miss Gillian?"

"Of course the older one," Katherine huffed. "She was the one he waltzed with and escorted into supper."

"I don't have a *fancy* for anyone," William shot back. "She was pleasant company. She likes horse riding."

There was another brief silence. Henry and Alexander shot a meaningful look which William did not like at all.

"I am not courting Miss Brookford," he said hotly. "I do not intend to court her. It's a serious decision, choosing the duchess of Dunleigh. Miss Bainbridge is the obvious choice."

And I have already agreed to marry her.

"That," Henry remarked contemplatively, "is a most intriguing manner of expressing it."

William felt the urge to scream in frustration. He was beginning to remember why he and his siblings didn't spend *too* much time together these days.

"Do elaborate."

"You don't speak of your future bride as your wife, your dearest friend, or even a partner in life. You talk about the next duchess of Dunleigh."

"What is your point? This is a decision based on logic. I am not falling in love, Henry."

Henry nodded thoughtfully. "We were all in accord regarding that sentiment."

William bit his lip. "I'm not like you three."

There was another silence. More meaningful looks were exchanged, and William began to feel as though he had compromised himself.

"I don't... I don't mean that as an insult," he managed at last, not looking anyone in the eye. "I... I've known for a long time that I am not an emotional man. I'm like him, aren't I? It's best that I allow logic and reason to dictate my choices. You three had the freedom to choose, but I'm the duke. I cannot simply do what I want. I have people who rely on me, an estate to run, and I need to be serious. Marrying a woman like Miss Bainbridge would be a good choice."

Katherine pursed her lips. "Explain."

William shrugged. "She's clever and efficient. She could handle social matters, run the house and part of the estate well. I could trust her. She'd bring a great deal of money along, allowing us to expand and improve the estate. She knows how to behave as a duchess, she knows what it is expected of her, and frankly, I think we'd work well together."

"How romantic," Henry observed, and Alexander gave a hoot of laughter.

"*You* can't talk about romance!" he laughed, shaking his head. "You're the least romantic person I have ever met."

"Eleanor thinks otherwise," Henry shot back, but Alexander was still laughing.

"Eleanor mirrors your disposition perfectly. She is earnest, businesslike, and candid. One might presume she perceives you as a romantic."

"Ugh. You are quite a simpleton, Kat. Proceed, it is your turn."

"I daresay I could afford to forgo a turn, truth be told," Katherine replied with a smirk. "I am currently in the lead."

They exploded into arguments, laughing and jesting. William said nothing, simply letting the atmosphere wash over him.

For a moment, he could pretend there were no guests at all, only perhaps his mother and his in-laws floating around the house. Just him and his siblings, laughing and jesting with each other, the way the old Duke had hated so much.

Why did he have to separate us so often? William caught himself wondering. *Did he believe that loving somebody, even one's spouse or siblings, was a sign of weakness? Did he think he was making us strong?*

William sometimes felt as though he understood his father rather too well. He believed that the answer was yes – the old Duke thought that isolation and hardship would make his children strong, able to withstand the world, able to live up to the exacting standards he thought they should achieve.

Well, he had made them strong, but not in the way he had imagined.

Katherine made her final shot, the winning shot, and leapt up and down in glee, billiard cue held above her head in triumph.

Henry complained loudly, Alexander laughed, and William allowed himself a small smile, etching the scene into his memory.

I love my family.

The moment was swiftly ruined. A light tap on the door made Katherine's triumphant crows fade away. She came back to herself, shaking out her skirts and putting on the face of a polite, passive lady.

A footman nervously shuffled into the room.

"Your Grace, the gentlemen in the dining room were asking for you."

William bit back a sigh. "I should join them. Thank you for the game, you three."

As he left the billiard room, he felt, oddly enough, as though he were leaving a piece of his heart behind.

Dukes can't care about hearts. Dukes have duty to consider.

Chapter Eight

Gillian was in high spirits, at least.

Lavinia smothered a yawn and tried to look interested. Her sister was thrilled to attend the Pump Room, the centre of Bath Society, where *everybody* went, and her mother was looking forward to taking the waters.

"It will give my health the boost it needs," Lady Brennon said, more than once, inspecting her complexion in a nearby mirror and giving a self-satisfied nod. "I wish we could persuade your father to come out with us. He has closeted himself in the library since he arrived."

"I'm sure Papa is enjoying himself quite enough," Lavinia said mildly, earning herself a grunt in response. "I've heard that sea-bathing is supposed to be more healthy than taking the waters."

She drew her knees up to her chest, perched as she was on the edge of her bed, and thought about that. Lavinia had never, of course, swam in the sea. What would it be like? Better than wallowing in a bath or even swimming in a pond. The sea was a living thing, full of other living things. *Powerful.*

"I should like to go sea-bathing," she remarked after a pause, thoughtfully.

Lady Brennon snorted. "Do not place your hopes upon it. We have only just managed to persuade your Papa to join us here, and I dare say that a sojourn at the seaside is not without considerable expense. I would advise you to partake of the waters while you still have the opportunity and leave the matter at that."

Lavinia sighed, banishing her dreams of sea-bathing. It was probably for the best. Given her customary fortune, she would no doubt be swept away by the tide regardless.

Gillian had finally settled on a gown, a frothy, pale green confection that suited her remarkably well. Lavinia was wearing a plain deep purple dress, along with her straw bonnet. Her mother glanced over the gown, thrown over the bottom of Lavinia's bed, and pursed her lips.

"Gillian, my dear, if you are prepared, perhaps you might descend to breakfast. Your sister and I shall join you momentarily."

"Oh, I don't mind waiting," Gillian said, oblivious.

Lady Brennon cleared her throat pointedly. "I insist, my dear. Off you go."

Gillian got the hint at last, throwing an apologetic look at her sister, and scuttled away. Lavinia uncurled herself from where she sat, feeling the first twinges of nerves.

"What is it, Mama? You look awfully serious."

Lady Brennon sniffed, fingering the long, grey ribbons Lavinia had put out to wear in her hair.

"You caused quite a stir, waltzing with the Duke. *And* then he escorted you into dinner and sat beside you."

Oh. This. I should have expected that Mama would not simply let this go. Lavinia bit her lip.

"He's just being a polite host, Mama. I know you wanted him to dance with Gillian, but she was *so* tired, and I believe he could see that."

"Indeed, well, what's done is done, there. I only say that it caused a stir because a great many people mentioned it. I overheard a few intriguing conversations, and some people even made attempts to draw me out."

"I am sorry, Mama," Lavinia said, not quite sure what else she was meant to say. "I'll try and avoid him, if I can."

Lady Brennon tsked. "No, *no,* you silly girl. Look. I have heard a rumour that the duke is *not* looking for a debutante." She raised her eyebrows expectantly.

Lavinia raised her eyebrows back. "Well, I should hope not. He's a grown man, is he not? He may even be close to thirty now. I cannot abide the sight of aged gentlemen pursuing the affections of young maidens of but seventeen years. It strikes me as rather inappropriate, in truth."

"Oh, my dear, you have no clue how Society works, but never mind. Don't you see? It means that the duke might not object to a spinster. Your age need not be a burden!"

"I never consider my age *as* a burden, Mama."

"You are an optimistic girl. I shall give you that. My point is," Lady Brennon sat down heavily on the bed beside her daughter, leaning close, "you have an *opportunity* here. Why not try to catch the duke?"

Lavinia should have seen this coming, of course. However, she found herself flinching away, chest tightening. She gave a nervous laugh.

"Mama, really! There is quite a competition going on for the duke's attention. You know how I hate to compete at anything."

"Be serious, please. He would not have waltzed with you if he had not liked you."

"Of course he would!" Lavinia wanted to laugh. "He is a kind man, and a gentleman. He would have waltzed with me to avoid offending me. Believe me, Mama, the duke feels nothing at all for me. I am his mother's guest – no, *you* are his mother's guest, and I am simply your daughter. I daresay he doesn't consider me from one moment to the next. Why should he?"

Lady Brennon pressed her lips together. "Perhaps I have been remiss in your training. My dear girl, men like the duke do not simply make their feelings known. I daresay he is trying to decide which lady would make the finest duchess –

that is something that must be considered – and you, my girl, are in his choices."

Lavinia got to her feet. "No, Mama, I am not. Miss Victoria Bainbridge has her eye on him, and how can I compete with her?"

Lady Brennon sniffed. "Easily, I should think. She could never match your beauty."

"She is clever, and rich, and confident. She has her eye on the duke, and frankly, she is the best choice. If he as logical as you say, why would he not choose her?"

Lady Brennon's eyes glinted. "So you *are* intrigued by the man, at the very least? You would consider trying to catch him?"

Lavinia gave a groan. "No, Mama, I would not."

How could she explain? Of course, the whole awful tale of their first meeting at Lady Clarissa's party would make her mother see that the duke was *not* interested in her and would not change his mind, but that would involve having to *tell* her mother what had happened.

Absolutely not.

"Mama, I really must get ready. I don't want to be late."

Lady Brennon huffed. "Fine. But think on what I said. If you could catch a duke, it would change our fortunes forever. I tried to push Gillian at him, but he barely looked at her twice."

On this cheery, maternal note, Lady Brennon swept out, slamming the door behind her.

***

The Pump Room was packed to the brim.

Lavinia had assumed – wrongly so, as it transpired – that mid-morning would be a pleasant, quiet time to take the waters and perhaps enjoy a cup of tea or two.

No.

The building itself was breathtaking – Lavinia was quite in love with the smooth white stone she saw everywhere, and the traditional Roman designs – and the assembly rooms were large and well-furnished. However, it seemed that this was the most fashionable time for Bath, and therefore the rooms were full.

They were required to sign in and elbowed their way through the crowds to find seats.

The Dowager Duchess accompanied them and walked arm in arm with Lady Brennon. Lavinia clutched her sister as though she might be torn away in the crush. She kept spotting a glimpse of broad shoulders, and a chestnut-curled head taller than the gentlemen.

That was him, of course. The duke. Try as she might, Lavinia was not quite able to restrain a shiver whenever he glanced her way. It was infuriating, but only to be expected. He *was* a rich and powerful man, who was also her host. His gaze was cool and level, almost unblinking, and really a woman would have to be blind to think him unattractive.

Stop it! she scolded herself, tightening her arm in Gillian's.

"Ouch, Lavvy. Don't pinch. I'm still tired from last night – do you think we shall find any seats?"

"We must," Lavinia said, shooting a quick glance at her sister. It had been close to dawn by the time they retired to bed last night. Their mother had not permitted them to go to bed early.

Well, perhaps Lavinia would have been allowed to go, but Gillian was very popular and a great many eligible gentlemen wanted to talk to her, so naturally Lady Brennon would not allow her to miss out on such opportunities. Lavinia chose to stay up, mostly to keep an eye on her sister.

The duke had not appeared after supper. When the gentlemen finally joined the ladies again, he was not there, and Lady Brennon managed to find out from the Dowager that he had played billiards and then gone to bed.

Privileged man, Lavinia had thought sourly at the time. She felt it even more now, since her eyes were gritty and heavy with sleep.

"Perhaps taking the water would do you good," she commented, eyeing her pale sister. "There's meant to be all kinds of goodness in it."

"I can't imagine that *water* is that healthy."

"Healthier than wine or port, certainly. Oh, there's a seat. Do make haste."

Lavinia dashed forward, manoeuvring Gillian into a single empty seat seconds before a large lady decorated with feathers could take the seat. The woman glared balefully at them both, and Lavinia smiled sweetly back until she moved off.

"Perhaps we should have let that woman sit here," Gillian murmured.

"You need to sit, Gillian. You must rest."

"But there's only one spare seat. Where will you sit?"

"Well, I don't need to sit right now. I am going to get us a glass of water each, and then we will sip it right here, and discuss its health benefits."

Gillian giggled when Lavinia pulled a face. "Well, very well. Please do not tarry overlong, as I would rather not be left to my own devices, particularly if that lady returns and casts an unfriendly glance my way; I fear I may be compelled to relinquish the seat to her."

"Don't you dare. I mean it. I shall be right back."

Lavinia scurried off through the crowd. She generally made better time by herself, without Gillian, because she utilized her elbows well enough to propel herself between people who would otherwise not think of moving out of the way of a young woman.

There was, unsurprisingly, a crowd near the pump, a harried attendant handing out glasses of cloudy water. Lavinia got to the counter and smiled winningly.

"Two glasses, please."

A figure materialised at her side, making her jump.

"Do you often take the water, Miss Brookford?" Miss Bainbridge asked sweetly. "I myself do not enjoy the taste. Besides, drinking *warm* water is never a pleasant experience."

"Not often," Lavinia managed. "But I thought it might do my sister some good. At least, it won't do her any *harm*."

Miss Bainbridge leaned her elbows on the counter, gesturing to the attendant that she wanted one glass. He sprang into action, much more enthusiastically than he had done for Lavinia.

"I must compliment you on your dancing, Miss Brookford. You waltz remarkably well."

Lavinia's cheeks burned. She glanced at the other woman, not sure whether she was being insulted or not.

"Thank you. I don't waltz often, so I am glad I remembered all the steps."

"I think it odd how unforgiving Society is when it comes to things such as dancing," Miss Bainbridge remarked, almost to herself. "If one misses a step, or stands on one's partner's foot – or, heaven forbid, *trips and falls* – everybody is shocked. It's the most natural thing to do in the world, to make a mistake, but we simply cannot abide it as a society. Strange, no?"

Lavinia shot the woman a long look. "I cannot help but feel that you are not talking about dancing at all, Miss Bainbridge."

The woman flashed her a wide, toothy grin, not the sort of demure smiles she generally preferred. Her round spectacles glinted.

"You are a clever woman, Miss Brookford. I admire that. Perhaps I ought to be frank."

"Yes, perhaps."

They were interrupted by the attendant sliding a glass of water towards Miss Bainbridge, who took it with a curl of her lip.

Lavinia, who had placed her order before Miss Bainbridge, glared at the attendant until he flushed red and turned back towards the pump.

"I intend to be Duchess of Dunleigh," Miss Bainbridge said at last. "I don't like to rely on wiles and cunning to achieve my ends. I have no skill in manipulation. I prefer logic, reason, and honesty, and I believe that the duke feels the same way. Frankly, I would make a good duchess. His Grace is not looking for a love match, but for somebody who would be an honour to his rank, and someone he can rely upon. I believe that such a position requires a great deal of responsibility, and I think I can fulfil those responsibilities. Can you declare the same for yourself?"

Lavinia stayed silent. Miss Bainbridge did not seem to expect an answer.

She drank back her glass of water in several long gulps, pulling a face at the taste, and set down the empty glass on the counter.

"Good day to you, Miss Brookford," she said quietly. "I hope your sister recovers well today. She looked tired last night."

Without another word, Miss Bainbridge glided away, her small form quickly swallowed up in the crowd.

The attendant set down two glasses of water without looking at Lavinia. Just as well, since she was glaring balefully at him.

It was something of an issue to get back through the crowd, clutching a glass of water in each gloved hand, but Lavinia managed it with her sharp elbows.

However, when she reached the place where she had left Gillian, she found the fat woman in the seat instead of her sister.

"Where is my sister?" Lavinia barked out, before she could help herself. "She was sitting here only a moment ago."

The woman turned up her nose and did not deign to answer, fluttering herself madly with a fan and hiding a self-satisfied smile. Abruptly, somebody behind Lavinia jostled her, and she slopped water all over her arm.

"Oh, *bother!*" Lavinia gasped aloud, in a most unladylike way. With impeccable timing, she turned and found herself face to face with none other than the Duke of Dunleigh himself, staring impassively down at her.

"Oh," she squeaked. "Your Grace."

Chapter Nine

William glanced at the trail of water soaking into Miss Brookford's glove, and hastily withdrew a handkerchief.

"It wasn't I who jostled you," he said suddenly, in case she thought he might have been responsible.

"I didn't think that it was you, your Grace," she responded, setting down the glasses on a nearby windowsill. "Where... where is my sister? I found her a seat, but apparently that woman persuaded her to give it up, and..."

"Oh, Miss Gillian went to sit with your mother, I believe. She asked me to let you know where she had gone. I believe she felt guilty at leaving you behind but found herself in great need of a chair." William paused, biting his lip. "Is Miss Gillian often unwell?"

Miss Brookford's expression tightened. "She's always been a little sickly. Not *too* sickly, but she requires a little extra care. I can look after her."

He nodded, hoping that he hadn't implied that she could *not* take care of her sister.

"Indeed, I'm sure of that. Does the water agree with you?"

She blinked, as if forgetting the very reason that Bath had been built, and snatched up one of the glasses, taking a long sip. Her nose wrinkled.

"Chalky. Warm and chalky."

He suppressed a smile. "That's meant to be a good sign."

"I'm sure it is. I feel healthier already."

He *did* laugh at that, smothering his smile with a hand. His father had been very clear on his opinion of dukes who laughed or smiled ingratiatingly. Miss Brookford, however, did not seem to think his laughter was uncalled for or an unmanly display, and only gave a small, satisfied smile.

"So, as this is my first time in Bath," she said, draining her glass and looking as though she would rather spit it all out again, "tell me, what else is there to do here beyond drink the water?"

"A great deal, actually. There are theatres, dining houses – some excellent ones, I can make recommendations if you would like – and there is a great deal of good society in town at the moment. I believe my mother had planned plenty of gatherings, balls, soirees and such for her guests, so you needn't worry about being bored."

"Oh, I wasn't implying that I would be bored," she said hastily. "As I say, I haven't been in Bath before."

"There are the Roman Baths next door," William offered. "The architecture is quite breathtaking, and I believe we could learn a great deal from the innovations of the Romans. To contemplate what a civilization so distant from our own has accomplished! The structures of the aqueducts alone are..." he trailed off, suddenly aware that he was babbling excitedly about the sort of thing ladies were not often interested in. He glanced down at Miss Brookford, trying to gauge if he were boring her.

She was looking up at him expectantly, waiting for him to continue.

"Go on," she said. "I am listening."

He felt colour rise to his cheeks. Of course, William's olive skin did not allow for much visible blushing, but still.

"We are planning a tour of the Roman Baths today," he heard himself say. "You ought to come with us."

This was not why he had approached her. This was not the reason at all.

The real reason was that William had decided that enough was enough. He had her locket in his pocket, wrapped in the same delicate strip of muslin which had protected it since he found it, and he had planned to hand it over to her once and for all.

"Here," he would say, as casually as possible, "I believe this is yours? I picked it up after a party, and I believe it belongs to you."

And then he would dismiss any expressions of gratitude, and the matter would be concluded.

Yet his hand remained resolutely out of his pocket, and Miss Brookford remained unaware that he had the necklace at all.

What is wrong with you? Just give it back. The longer you keep it, the odder it will look. Give the wretched thing back, and then you can concentrate on more important matters, like managing the future and letting Miss Bainbridge know her plans are acceptable.

I daresay the woman already has our wedding planned out, down to the guest list.

It was half a joke, but suddenly didn't seem very funny at all.

"Your Grace?"

He blinked, suddenly jerked back to the present. Miss Brookford was looking up at him, mildly curious.

"Hm?"

"You seem preoccupied. Is..." she paused, shifting, "is everything quite alright, your Grace? Is there anything I can help with?"

Before William had a chance to say anything at all – not that he had the slightest idea of what he *might* say – Alexander came sailing over, with Abigail on his arm.

"Enjoying the water?" Alexander chirped. "Good day, Miss Brookford."

"I believe Lady Brennon said that this is your first visit to Bath?" Abigail spoke up, as softly spoken as always. She had come out of her shell since her marriage to Alexander, but she was still Abigail, who thought before she spoke and never had a harsh word for anybody. Frankly, William thought that his brother had met with exceptional good luck in marrying Abigail, although Society in general had disapproved of the match for many reasons. For example, Alexander had a reputation as a rake, and Abigail and her family were not wealthy.

Not that it mattered, of course. After his wedding, Alexander received his portion of their inheritance and was now a remarkably rich man. The only part of the Willenshire inheritance that was not claimed was William's part. He was receiving increasingly nervous letters from the family solicitor, reminding him of the terms of the will and the approaching deadline.

As if I wasn't aware of every passing day, launching me towards the deadline, William thought, with a rush of frustration. *As if I don't have my siblings' happy marriages in front of me constantly, reminding me of what I do not have and will likely never achieve.*

Not marriage, of course, I'm fairly sure I can manage that.

Love.

He swallowed hard, jerking himself back to the present.

"His Grace was just telling me that you plan a tour of the Roman Baths today," Miss Brookford was saying, and William was uncomfortably aware that the conversation had gone on without him. Nobody had noticed, however.

No, that was not quite true. He glanced up and saw his sister-in-law looking at him, her expression thoughtful and cool. She gave him a small smile, and he was not entirely sure what it meant. Or even *if* it meant anything.

"You ought to come with us," Alexander was saying. "King's Bath, isn't it? That's what we're touring? The ladies are doing the Queen's Bath."

Abigail shot her husband a quick, intent look which William could not interpret, but Alexander's eyebrows flickered.

"You should come with us to the King's Bath," he said at once, before William could say a word.

William bit his lip. Hard. "Alexander, I'm sure Miss Brookford would rather…"

"Oh, yes, I would love to!" she chirped, before he could finish. "His Grace was just telling me about the architecture and the cleverness of the Romans, and I should love to see it myself in person. My mother and sister will probably be happy to while away their afternoon here in the Pump Room, but I am already bored." She paused, blinking. "Not *bored*, exactly. Ladies aren't bored, are they?"

Colour rushed into her face, but she recovered when Abigail reached over and patted her shoulder.

"I know it," she said soothingly. "Don't worry – this is quite an informal gathering. The Dowager likes things done properly, but when it's just us, things are quite different. I was pleasantly surprised by how friendly the Willenshire siblings are. You'll find the same, I'm sure."

William eyed his sister-in-law. *Save the charm for Miss Bainbridge,* he wanted to say. *She's the one we want to impress.*

Miss Brookford smiled. "Thank you. I must say, all of this is quite new to me. Bath, and all that. I've never much enjoyed the Season."

Abigail exchanged a smiling look with Alexander. "Neither did I. Let me tell you, having the right person by your side makes all the difference."

Miss Brookford's smile faltered, just a little. She did not look at anyone in particular.

Before the awkward moment could expand, Lady Brennon appeared, elbowing her way through the crowd.

"There you are, Lavinia! Where in the world have you been?" she hissed, her grim expression softening to a smile when she saw William. "Oh, your Grace! I had no idea Lavinia was speaking to you. I thought she had become lost in reverie or some similarly fanciful notion. You know how capricious young ladies can be."

"That is not my experience, Lady Brennon," William managed, but the woman did not seem to be listening, entirely preoccupied with picking at the lace at Miss Brookford's neckline, and tweaking curls into place. "Please, don't let me keep you."

"His Grace has invited me to tour the Roman Baths afterwards," Miss Brookford said, determination in her voice. "The King's Baths, I believe."

Lady Brennon blinked. "The *King's* Baths? Don't you mean the Queen's Baths? Oh, never mind, it hardly matters. Of course you can go, dear. Now, come, Gillian is asking for you, and we are sitting with Mr. Thompson and his very genteel brother. Come along."

She towed her daughter into the crowd, whispering something into her ear that bore a notable resemblance to the adage, "do not place all your eggs in a single basket."

That left the three of them alone. Abigail and Alexander both turned to level slow, thoughtful looks at William.

He bit the inside of his cheek. "What are you two looking at? And while we're at it, Alexander, what *were* you thinking? Ladies tour the Queen's Bath, and gentlemen tour the King's. Why would you invite Miss Brookford to come with us?"

Alexander shrugged. "Abigail wanted me to."

"How in the world did you know that she... oh, never mind. You shouldn't have done that. Miss Brookford doesn't know how things are done."

"It's not as if she'll be ruined, touring the King's Baths," Abigail sighed. "It's just a silly tradition. I suspect that Miss Brookford would be interested in seeing both Baths, to be truthful."

Alexander narrowed his eyes, taking a step closer to William. "And I suspect that my brother is more interested in Miss Brookford than he cares to let on."

"Yes, I suspect so too," Abigail said, eyeing him absently. "It is harder than you might imagine, following your heart, William."

William cleared his throat, straightening his waistcoat. The conversation had suddenly become too uncomfortable, and the crowds were pressing in on him in a way he had not noticed before.

"I have made up my mind, almost. Miss Bainbridge is the obvious choice for my bride. She is educated, well-bred, and can manage the role perfectly. I would be a simpleton to look elsewhere."

"I have to agree," Alexander shrugged. "I don't particularly like Miss Bainbridge, but I think she would suit *you*, William."

That sounded like an insult, somehow, but William kept his lips closed and said nothing.

You don't know me; he found himself thinking. *And neither does Miss Bainbridge.*

Chapter Ten

The King's Bath was truly beautiful. Lavinia took in every detail, awestruck, and wished she'd thought to bring a notebook. Or, better yet, a sketchbook. She was not skilled at watercolours, but she could produce a serviceable sketch, if the situation called for it. It would be pleasant to sketch some of the architecture and look over them once she was back home.

The thought of home made her feel uneasy, for some reason. If the Season went well, Gillian would make a remarkable match and would never probably come home again.

I'll be alone. Just Mama, Papa and me. There'll be no need to come to London anymore, or attend the Season, as there's no likelihood that I'll marry.

I'm going to be so alone.

Misery tightened her chest, almost making her breathless for a moment or two. She swallowed hard, bringing herself back down to the present.

There were mostly men touring the King's Baths. Lavinia had realized that there was a tradition about the tours – men toured the King's Baths, and women toured the Queen's Baths. There were a few women here, of course, notably Lady Abigail Willenshire, Katherine, and, to Lavinia's dismay, Miss Bainbridge.

Often, Lavinia felt eyes bore into her back, her neck itching, and she would turn to find Miss Bainbridge averting her eyes. It was the first time she had ever seen the woman even a little discomfited.

She was not sure she liked it. Miss Bainbridge was well-known in the higher circles of Society, being both rich, intelligent, and confident. Some men pretended to turn up their nose at her, finding fault in her character, face, or form, but everybody knew that if she flashed them a smile, they would come running to her. Miss Bainbridge struck Lavinia as the sort of woman who could have anything she wanted and knew it very well.

Am I jealous of her? Lavinia thought, allowing herself a small smile. *Yes, I believe so. I suppose it is a compliment to Miss Bainbridge, in a way. I have no idea what I could have done to make her dislike me, though. Have I offended her in some way?*

She was inspecting a crumbling aqueduct with a sculpture looming above it when a familiar figure came to stand beside her.

"I came here when I was a boy," the duke said, eyes fixed on the sculpture. "I thought it remarkably beautiful. I would have stayed for hours, I think, but my father got tired of the place rather quickly, and so we left. I suppose I could have come back any time I liked, once he was gone, but somehow, I never did. Isn't that odd?"

Lavinia pursed her lips. "Habits can be deeply ingrained, as can some beliefs. Perhaps if your father thought this place was not worth seeing, you somehow believed it yourself."

He gave a short, mirthless laugh. "It didn't stop me from buying and devouring books about Roman architecture and the Roman Baths, though."

"Well, that's different from coming here, is it not? My mother believes that novels are a waste of time, and nothing but silliness. That doesn't prevent me from enjoying them, but whenever my sister tries to read them, she says that she can't seem to enjoy them herself. I know that it isn't simply her own preference, because before Mama told us what she thought about novels, she liked reading them very much."

"I suppose that if somebody you admire and respect has a low opinion on something, it is hard not to share it," the duke said, still staring thoughtfully at the sculpture.

"And love."

He blinked down at her, missing a beat. "Hm?"

"And love. Somebody you admire, respect... and love. That's a rather crucial part of the story, don't you think?"

The duke looked at her for a second or two, expression unreadable.

"Yes, of course," he said at last, but there was something odd in his voice, something that Lavinia could not interpret.

She was beginning to feel out of her depth. All of this – Bath, the architecture, the company, the houses – belonged to people above her.

This is not my circle. They are not my people. She glanced up at the duke, who was now looking at the sculptures again. He didn't seem to be truly *seeing* them, though. There was a furrow between his brows, making him look oddly younger and more vulnerable. A wave of affection rolled through Lavinia, no matter how hard she tried to stamp it down and remind herself that this was not a *proper* feeling. She wanted to wind an arm around his broad shoulders and pull him down for an embrace, reassuring him that everything would be fine, absolutely fine.

These are not his people, either. I suppose he is just more used to pretending.

He is afraid.

As if to highlight her fears a little more, Miss Bainbridge appeared.

"There you are, your Grace," she said, smiling easily. "And Miss Brookford, too! I am surprised to see you here. I might have thought that the Queen's Bath would be more to your taste."

"I haven't seen either of the Baths," Lavinia answered, managing a cool smile. "I would like to see the Queen's Baths, too. There's a great deal I would like to see in Bath."

Miss Bainbridge chuckled benignly. "Yes, I forget that you don't come here every year. Why don't you, by the way? It's very fashionable to keep a house in Bath these days. We have our own townhouse, naturally. Bath is so very refreshing after the heat and bustle of London."

Lavinia laughed uncertainly. "I'm not quite sure why we don't have a house here. Perhaps my parents don't believe we'd use it enough. It would be quite wasted."

"Wasted? Not at all. All you would require is a modest staff to oversee matters, and you could keep it closed for the greater part of the year. The expenditure would be quite minimal. I trust you are indeed mindful of the costs, naturally."

She added the last part gently, almost regretfully. Lavinia's face burned.

Of course, it was fairly clear that her family could *not* afford a house in Bath. They couldn't even afford a house in London, and it was growing increasingly likely that they would not be able to afford their country house, either. That was a particular worry that Lavinia was trying her utmost to ignore.

She wasn't entirely sure how Miss Bainbridge could know the full extent of their situation, but the tight, mirthless smile on her face seemed to indicate that she did. Lavinia glanced up at the duke, bewildered, not entirely sure how to respond, not sure what veiled insults she was missing.

The duke pressed his lips together. "I can't say I agree with this modern idea of keeping half a dozen houses in various parts of the country," he said suddenly. Miss Bainbridge shot him a sharp look, which he pretended to ignore. "What good can it possibly do? The expense – forgive me for saying, Miss Bainbridge – is truly shocking, and for what benefit? A house in town and a house in the country is quite enough for any family, in my opinion."

There was a faint pause after this. Lavinia was vaguely aware that the duke had just corrected a lady, which of course was not at all the proper thing to do.

Miss Bainbridge spoke next.

"I suppose you are right," she said at last. Her voice was light and almost careless, but there was a hard look in her eyes which Lavinia did not like. "Let us just change the subject. Tell me, your Grace, but do these sculptures not remind you of a particular gallery in Italy? I cannot recall the name, but I am sure you have visited it on your Grand Tour."

Lavinia felt like sinking into the floor. It was fairly clear that Miss Bainbridge was trying to push her out of the conversation, and frankly it was working. She had never travelled abroad, never gone anywhere further than Scotland. She'd never seen Paris, or Italy, or Spain, or Germany. She'd barely managed to go to London once a year.

However, in the silence that followed, it became clear that Miss Bainbridge had mis-stepped.

"You are mistaken, Miss Bainbridge," the duke said, his voice cold. "I never had a Grand Tour."

The woman blinked, looking a little disconcerted. "Oh, I was sure..."

"No, never. Do excuse me, ladies."

Abruptly, the duke turned on his heel and strode away, leaving the two women standing side by side, both red-faced.

Miss Bainbridge bit back an unladylike curse which had Lavinia convinced that her ears were playing tricks on her.

"His father, of course."

"I beg your pardon?" Lavinia said, bewildered.

Miss Bainbridge waved her hand. "The old duke was quite mad, everybody knows that. He ruled his family with an iron fist. He allowed the second Willenshire boy – Henry – to travel a little, and *he* had a Grand Tour. I can't recall if Alexander went abroad. I think not, but it hardly matters. His Grace has not travelled abroad at all. I cannot believe that I was so foolish as to forget that."

Lavinia said nothing. The Grand Tour was generally seen as a proof of one's manliness, almost a rite of passage. It made sense that the duke would be uncomfortable about not taking a Tour.

"It wasn't your fault," she found herself saying, trying to reassure her. "It was just a mistake."

Miss Bainbridge breathed in deeply, straightening her shoulders. She turned to look at Lavinia with a cool smile.

"Perhaps so. But I should warn you, my dear, that I do not make mistakes very frequently. Remember that."

Without waiting for a response, she turned and strode away, leaving Lavinia with the sinking feeling that, once again, she was well out of her depth.

Chapter Eleven

"I suppose that if somebody you admire and respect has a low opinion on something, it is hard not to share it."

"And love."

"Hm?"

"And love. Somebody you admire, respect... and love. That's a rather crucial part of the story, don't you think?"

It was almost time to go down for dinner, and yet William was sitting on the edge of his bed, staring into space, shoulders hunched. He kept replaying the conversation he'd had with Miss Brookford over and over in his head.

There'd been more conversations beyond that particular one, but always painfully polite, always with other people involved.

What are you doing? He asked himself angrily. *You've decided. It is decided. You have an agreement of honour with the lady. Miss Bainbridge is the woman for you. She'll be a perfect duchess. So why spend all of this time worrying about Lavinia Brookford? Miss Bainbridge made it clear she wasn't pleased with you talking to her so excessively. Why upset your future wife?*

It made sense, after all. Miss Bainbridge was the one who he had agreed to marry. Perhaps the decision had been made in haste, but it wasn't as if he could withdraw his consent now. A deal had been made, and no gentleman would renege on such an agreement. And really, she *was* the best choice.

Perhaps if he kept repeating it to himself, he would finally start to believe it.

With a sigh, William dragged himself to his feet. He had dismissed his valet in order to think more clearly, and yet he hadn't managed to really *think* about anything at all.

William had more or less given up on becoming attracted to Miss Bainbridge. She was pretty enough, for sure, and intelligent, and perfect in all respects for the role she so clearly wanted. And yet he felt nothing towards her.

He wondered if she knew. Probably. She was a clever woman, after all, and very intuitive.

Did she mind? He imagined not. After all, a husband who was not actually *in love with* his wife was more likely to leave her alone, and Miss Bainbridge struck him as the kind of woman who liked to be left alone.

It was also apparent that she did not like Miss Lavinia Brookford.

It seemed pointless to deny, at least in his own head, that he found himself drawn to Miss Brookford. William wasn't entirely sure what it was that attracted him so strongly to her, or why he had not yet given the wretched locket back to the woman, but nevertheless the feelings were there.

He wished they would go away. Miss Brookford was not part of the plan. William's plan was a carefully laid one, and he did not intend to go astray. Miss Brookford was... was something else, to be sure, but she would not make a good duchess. Not without a great deal of work, and William needed a duchess.

He stared bleakly at himself in the mirror. He already knew how the dinner table seats had been laid out, and he was sitting directly next to Miss Bainbridge.

"It makes perfect sense," he said aloud. "Perfect sense."

***

Billiard balls scuttled across the green baize tabletop, skidding towards the pockets in the corner. The ball William had been aiming at missed the pocket, bouncing off the side and ricocheting back towards him. He bit back a curse and readjusted his position for a second shot.

"Goodness, you're terrible at this time."

William flinched, banging his knee on the underside of the table. He twisted around, squinting at his sister.

"Go away, Katherine. You're meant to be sitting with the ladies in the drawing room."

"And *you* are meant to be in the dining room still, drinking port with the gentlemen and laughing genteelly at unfunny jokes. Why are you in here, playing billiards by yourself?"

He bit his lip. "I have a migraine."

She narrowed her eyes, leaning forward. "Lies. I can always tell when you're lying, you know. And I can always tell when you have a migraine – your eyes become all misty and rimmed with crimson. You don't have a migraine."

A flash of bad temper rolled through William. He took up a position again, aiming for the same ball as before. He wasn't exactly playing the game properly, just hitting balls almost at random, waiting for... well, he wasn't sure what he was waiting for.

"I wanted a little time to myself. Is that too much to ask? My house is full of guests, none of which were invited by me, and I am expected to spend all day and half of the night entertaining them. It's overwhelming, Kat. It's nearly unbearable."

There was a brief silence, and William wished he hadn't spoken so loudly.

"Your house," Katherine repeated, after a pause.

He sighed. "You know what I mean."

"I know that you inherited everything, but I thought that we would all be united. Wasn't that what we agreed? If one of us couldn't get married, we'd take care of each other either way?"

He bit his lip, straightening slowly. The balls clipped and clacked their way across the table. He missed again.

"Yes," he murmured, feeling oddly ashamed. "Yes, I remember that we agreed that. You know what I mean, though, Katherine."

She folded her arms. "I'm not entirely sure that I do, you know. Lately, you've been acting stranger than ever."

"What do you mean, stranger than ever? I am myself."

Katherine snorted. "Well, Miss Bainbridge is stamping around in the drawing room, waiting for you to arrive. She's been insufferable today. Have you said something to her?"

"Why do you assume it's my fault?" William shot back. His temper was hanging by a thread, and he was determined not to have an outburst. He might possess a striking resemblance to their father, but he swore he would not comport himself in the same manner.

"William, when she arrived here, she was cool and calm and entirely at ease. She seemed secure of you. Now she's... well, a little on edge. She's snapping at her family, being disagreeable to the other guests, and seems to be trying to chase you around the house. Whatever has happened, she's not quite as sure of you as she was before. If you've changed your mind about her, it would be better to put her out of her misery."

He sighed, raking a hand through his hair. The billiard balls were scattered all over the table, but he didn't feel much of a desire to finish his odd little game.

"I have not changed my mind. It's just..."

Katherine waited patiently for him to collect his thoughts. William stared at the colourful billiard balls until his eyes blurred.

"I am engaged to Miss Bainbridge," he blurted out.

Katherine's eyes bulged. "*What*? You proposed to her?"

"She proposed to me, actually," he mumbled, and launched into a description of their strange meeting together, although he omitted how he had met Miss Brookford directly afterwards. Katherine's brows drew together as he spoke.

"It's not an official engagement," she said slowly. "One might argue that you weren't really *bound*."

"Come, come, Kat, that's not true. I am honour-bound to the woman. It's just that I do not love her," he said at last, the words small and tight. "I'm a fool to want love."

"You aren't a fool. Oh, Will, I had no idea."

He swallowed thickly. "You can't tell anyone. Not yet."

"I won't, Will, you know I won't. I must tell Timothy, though – have I your permission to that? He's the soul of discretion."

He nodded, and Katherine crossed the space between them and folded her arms around him. William closed his eyes, resting his chin on his sister's shoulder, and letting himself sink into the embrace.

Just for a moment, though.

He cleared his throat, straightening up and gently pushing Katherine away. Disappointment crossed her face, quickly erased, but he still saw it.

"You can't marry her, Will," she said, voice quiet. "Miss Bainbridge, I mean. I know that you have a bargain with her, but can't you consider your happiness at all? Miss Brookford is..."

"Enough about Miss Brookford," he said shortly. "She won't make a good duchess. I can't consider her as a wife, even if she were interested in me. Which, by the way, I assume that she is not. As for my happiness, I must be the best judge of that, mustn't I? Please don't talk about it, Katherine."

Katherine gave a tight, annoyed sigh. "Very well, very well. You always did do as you liked, William. I shall let you manage your own happiness, then, but remember this – it is very important to all of us that you *are* happy, do you understand?"

William pressed his lips together. "I shall be happy if I can do my duty."

There was a brief pause after this. He knew at once that he'd made a mistake."

"Father used to say that, didn't he?" Katherine said, her tone off-handed and deceptively light. "I hope you aren't letting his lessons and rules shape your choice of wife, William."

"Of course not. But... well, he wasn't *always* wrong, was he?"

Katherine only stared at him, holding his gaze until he looked away.

"That man," she said at last, "has overshadowed our lives for years. He drove Henry out of the country, nearly broke Alexander, nearly broke me, and you... well, William, you are unrecognizable from the boy I knew and loved when we were children."

"I'm sorry I am such a disappointment to you," he snapped, but Katherine darted towards him, gripping his shoulders and turning him to face her.

"You are a not a *disappointment*, I just know that if you'd been raised by kind, good parents, you would be a different man now. A happier one, less anxious, more carefree. I want you to be *happy*, Will! Why is it hard for you to believe me?"

Avoiding her eye, William carefully brushed away her hands and stepped past her towards the door.

"As I said, Katherine. I will be happy when I can do my duty. Dukes are not destined for happiness. The sooner you accept that, the easier life will become. I have accepted it myself." He paused at the door, finally glancing back at her. "You should go back to the ladies in the drawing room. We gentlemen will join you presently."

He didn't wait for a response, simply slipped out into the cool, dark hallway.

Katherine did not follow him.

***

In the dining room, the seating arrangement had been abandoned. The gentlemen had mostly moved up to one end of the table, now that the ladies between them had gone, and were leaning towards each other in clusters. The air was heavy with cigar smoke, the table sticky with spilled brandy.

When William slipped into the room, he noticed several footmen shifting from foot to foot, stifling yawns and waiting for the opportunity to clear the table.

Most of the guests were deep in conversation, and did not notice William entering the room again.

With a few exceptions, of course.

Henry, who was still sitting opposite his brother, glanced sharply up, eyes narrowed.

"Where did you go?" he asked, as William lowered himself into his seat. "Are you alright?"

"Quite well, thank you," William lied smoothly. Henry did not seem convinced, but did not press further, thankfully.

Feeling eyes on him, he glanced down the table and saw none other than Mr. Bainbridge staring at him. The man offered a frosty smile, and almost immediately abandoned his seat in favour of an empty one directly beside William.

Oh, wonderful, William thought tiredly. *I might as well have gone to join the ladies right away, or else stayed in the billiards room.*

"Fabulous party, your Grace," Mr. Bainbridge said, smiling cheerfully. He was a tall, almost cadaverous-looking man, with a hawkish nose and the same sharp, sparkling eyes as his daughter. He was known as a man of few words and unbelievably deep pockets.

"Thank you, Mr. Bainbridge. I'm sorry you did not feel ready for a tour of the Baths earlier today."

"Yes, well, my wife and I attend Bath regularly for the water, you know. I've seen it all and done it all. In fact, I would say that there isn't a great deal that surprises Mrs. Bainbridge and me."

This felt like a pointed comment, and William was growing more uncomfortable by the minute. He flashed the man a tense smile.

"Quite right, I suppose," he said, in the hopes that this uninviting comment would stop the conversation in its tracks.

He should have known better. Mr. Bainbridge gestured for a footman to refill his brandy glass. He swirled the liquid round and round in the glass, holding it up to the light.

"A fine vintage, this," he said at last, taking a long sniff. "I can always tell. I have a palate for such things, you know. I can sniff out a liar as easily as I can a corked wine."

William didn't bother smiling at this. "How useful for you."

"Indeed, it is. My dear Victoria – my daughter, you know – is much the same. A clever little thing, she is. We have high hopes for her."

William tensed. "She is certainly a remarkably intelligent woman. I am often surprised by her intellect."

"Hm. You don't strike me as a man who would underestimate a woman."

"I am not."

"My Victoria is a clever girl. Cleverer than folks give her credit for, in fact. Once she's got her mind set on something, she gets it. Always. She's our only child, of course, and I recall that when she was young, people tended to say things about how much we must have wished she were a boy. I always laughed at them and told them they had no clue of what they were speaking. Boy or girl, Victoria is a force of nature. We never wished we had a son – not in her place, at least – and we never imagined that she was any less than she is."

The conversation was growing more and more pointed, and William longed to fidget in his seat. Mr. Bainbridge was staring at him with those pale, unblinking eyes, cutting through all the layers of William's excuses and concerns, all the way through to the vulnerable nerve underneath.

It wasn't a pleasant experience.

"You are a good father, I think," William said at last. "Miss Bainbridge is worthy of you."

"She is worthy of the best in the world," Mr. Bainbridge said, and there was a hint of sourness in his voice now. "The best food, clothes, friends, future. The best husband."

"I am inclined to agree."

"Anyone who trifles with her affections... forgive me, with her *expectations*... will find himself regretting his actions."

William could not let this one go. He shifted in his seat, looking Mr. Bainbridge full in the face.

"I am not sure why you are telling me this, Mr. Bainbridge. It almost feels like a threat."

Mr. Bainbridge narrowed his eyes. "You understand me well, your Grace, I think."

"No gentleman would make a promise he did not intend to keep, I think. However, that also means that a gentleman must be careful about what promises he *does* make, and how he extends them. Don't you agree?"

Mr. Bainbridge seemed to take his meaning at last. He said nothing, only blinking slowly, like a cat.

William had had more than enough. Glancing across the table, he found Henry still looking at him, his eyes sharp. William rose to his feet, and the other gentlemen glanced over at him, their conversations faltering away.

"I think it is time to let the long-suffering servants get into the dining room," William said, with a wry smile. "They have waited long enough. Come, shall we join the ladies?"

There was a general murmur of assent, accompanied by the sound of chairs scraping upon the floor as gentlemen set down their glasses draining the final remnants of their brandy. They moved languidly towards the door, and William was one of the last men out of the dining room.

Not quite *the* last, though. When he glanced over his shoulder, Mr. Bainbridge was only just getting up from his seat, and his gaze was firmly fixed on William's retreating back.

Chapter Twelve

Generally, Lavinia hated the part of the evening where the gentlemen and ladies separated. The ladies always retreated to a parlour or the drawing room, to talk genteelly and occupy themselves, while the gentlemen indulged their desire for brandy and smoked cigars.

It wasn't that Lavinia disliked the company of other ladies in the slightest. It was just that many of the *other* ladies spent the time eyeing their rivals and waiting in scarcely veiled impatience for the gentlemen to return. More than once, Lavinia had seen a pair of young women fighting fiercely for the attention of some weak-chinned lord, only to put up a pretence of friendship during the interlude between dinner and the return of the gentlemen.

It was sickening, frankly.

This time, she had another concern. Gillian.

Gillian was visibly tired, and had been all day, and now she was fighting back yawn after yawn. A pair of ladies stood with her near the mantelpiece, side by side, talking about something or other. It meant that Gillian could not sit without breaking off the conversation, and of course she would rather collapse than be impolite. The heat of the fire had to be burning into her, and Lavinia saw a flush spreading over her sister's neck and collar.

The ladies only glanced briefly at her and continued their rattling on about whatever it was they were discussing. Lavinia had been introduced to the two women, of course, and had an idea that they were cousins, although she could not remember their names. They hadn't seemed particularly pleasant to her, and doubtless saw Gillian as a staunch rival.

It's no good. I must intervene. I must do something.

Just as the idea was taking root in Lavinia's head, and she was looking about for inspiration, Katherine came striding back into the room. When had she left?

She glanced around the room, and immediately her gaze came to rest on Gillian.

"Goodness, Miss Gillian, you are standing far too close to that fire! You'll faint from the heat! Miss Susan, Miss Anne, do you not see that the poor girl is flushed all over?"

Things happened quickly after that. Katherine escorted Gillian to a seat, while Miss Susan and Miss Anne protested innocence and claimed that *they* were not affected by the heat. Gillian was soon sitting on a long sofa, with Lady Abigail and Lady Eleanor on one side, and Katherine on the other. Lavinia watched as a normal colour returned to her sister's cheeks, and she relaxed in a calm and soothing conversation.

Those Willenshires are remarkably nice people, Lavinia thought, sinking back into her seat in relief. *Nicer than I would have expected.*

Her reprieve did not last. No sooner had Lavinia begun to relax again then she spotted none other than Miss Bainbridge, heading her way with an icy smile on her face.

Oh, good heavens. What have I done to deserve this?

"Do you mind if I sit by you, Miss Brookford?" Miss Bainbridge asked sweetly, taking a seat. "May I call you Lavinia?"

"Of course."

Miss Bainbridge did not suggest that Lavinia should call her Victoria. Lavinia thought about asking and decided against it.

The sofa was a two-seater, and the half not occupied by Lavinia was occupied by a large, fluffy white cat, curled up into a ball. Miss Bainbridge made an impatient gesture, and the cat leapt down with a growl of annoyance. She took its place, picking at her cuffs and readjusting her skirts.

Lavinia stayed silent. Something had undoubtedly driven the woman over here, and she would wait patiently to hear it.

"The gentlemen are taking their time to join us, are they not?" Miss Bainbridge said, at last.

Lavinia smiled weakly. "I hadn't noticed. I quite enjoy it when it's just us women, you know."

"Oh, really? I quite despise the company of women. They never have anything interesting to say."

"They? Don't you mean *we*? You're a woman too, Miss Bainbridge."

Miss Bainbridge only smiled absently. "In body only, I think you'll find."

Lavinia considered asking what on earth that was supposed to mean, but once again decided against speaking.

I'm getting quite shrewd these days, she thought, allowing herself a small smile. *Keeping my mouth shut at opportune moments.*

"His Grace, the Duke, is a remarkably kind man, don't you think?" Miss Bainbridge said at last, her gaze still fixed on a distant point across the room.

Lavinia hadn't been expecting this and found herself somewhat thrown by the comment.

"Hm? Yes, I suppose so."

"You *suppose* so? Why, you've been the recipient of his kindness since you arrived!"

Lavinia blinked, beginning to feel uncomfortable. "Do you mean his hospitality?"

Miss Bainbridge chuckled. "Oh, you are sweet. Gentlemen like the duke are rather practised in seeking out... oh, how shall I say this?... the most *unfortunate* in their society. You know, older widows, frumpy spinsters, gawky debutantes who haven't a clue how to act or what to say. The sort of woman that *nobody* would expect to marry a duke, which means that his reputation is quite safe. He'll be kind to her, make sure she is comfortable, make sure nobody is unpleasant to her, and so on. Like a charity endeavour, you know. People will follow a duke's lead, after all."

There was an unpleasant little silence between them.

"Forgive me," Lavinia said at last, "but I really don't understand what you are trying to say, Miss Bainbridge."

Miss Bainbridge gave a forced titter of laughter. "You are so sweet, Lavinia. Let me be plain, because I don't wish for you to embarrass yourself more than you have already done. Let me assure you that his Grace is not pursuing you for matrimonial reasons."

Colour rushed into Lavinia's face. "Well, I didn't think that he was."

"It's just that you are… oh, how shall I say it? You are pursuing him. It's a little unbecoming. He is trying to be kind, trying to put you at your ease, and… well, it's clear that you have misinterpreted his kindness. I am only telling you this because *somebody* must, my dear. With the greatest respect to dear Lady Brennon, it seems that she is entirely concentrating on pushing poor Miss Gillian and you towards the single gentlemen of our party. She's made a determined set, and people are beginning to notice. Oh, now I've upset you."

With a mournful expression that barely concealed a triumphant grin, Miss Bainbridge reached out and laid her hand on Lavinia's. The sharp edge of one of her nails dug sharply into Lavinia's knuckles. She couldn't tell whether it was deliberate or simply an accident.

"My mother is not pushing me towards anyone," Lavinia said at last. She couldn't quite believe what Miss Bainbridge had said.

Is it true? Is this some sort of high-Society politeness that I am not receiving properly? I certainly never imagined he could feel anything for me. I am a spinster, and he is a duke, and the most eligible man of the Season.

"Mm-hm," Miss Bainbridge said, smiling disbelievingly. "I just would hate for you to start thinking of him with hope, you know. When there is none. None at all, I'm afraid. The duke and I have an understanding, and a betrothal announcement is forthcoming."

Lavinia only smiled tightly and murmured something congratulatory. It did not deceive Miss Bainbridge, of course, but it concerned merely the appearance of matters.

Why should it matter what I think of him, in the privacy of my own head?

Miss Bainbridge lifted an eyebrow when the moments dragged on.

"Don't you want to thank me, Lavinia?" she said, voice gentle.

"Thank you for telling me, Miss Bainbridge," Lavinia managed, hating herself even as the words exited her mouth.

"You are most welcome, my dear, most welcome. As I said, I should hate to see you embarrass yourself more than you have already."

"Do retract your claws, you disagreeable little creature, or I shall be compelled to send you sprawling across the chamber."

There was an icy moment of silence at Lady Brennon's voice. Both women twisted to look up at the woman, who was standing directly behind the chair, hands on her hips.

"I *beg* your pardon?" Miss Bainbridge managed. Her voice was clipped and icy.

Lady Brennon smiled sweetly. "I was speaking to the cat, my dear."

All three of them glanced at the recently dislodged white cat, who was sitting a little way away, its claws notably not out.

"I see," Miss Bainbridge said, sounding irritated.

"Would you mind giving up your seat to an old woman, Miss Bainbridge? I would love to sit by my daughter, you know."

Miss Bainbridge smiled, tight-lipped, and rose without another word. She sailed off, never once glancing back, and Lady Brennon dropped into the seat beside Lavinia.

The cat came running up, leaping on Lady Brennon's lap. It curled up at once, purring hard, and she began to absently stroke it.

"You weren't talking about the cat, were you, Mama?" Lavinia said, after a pause.

"Of course not. I would never harm a cat."

Lavinia bit back a smile. "You don't want to make an enemy of Miss Bainbridge."

"It seems that you already have."

Lavinia's smile faded. "You heard what she said, then."

"I did, and I was furious. I hope you didn't believe anything she said."

"Well..." Lavinia glanced down at her lap, where her fingers were knotted tightly together. "I *am* a spinster, and a poor one at that. He has been remarkably kind to me, but I'd be a fool to take his kindness for anything other than plain old politeness."

Lady Brennon shifted to face her. "Now, you listen to me, girl. I am not the finest mother in the world, and I know that... that sometimes I focus a little too much on Gillian."

"I know, I know, you don't have to remind me."

"But let me tell you this. I know more of the world than you, *and* more than little Miss Bainbridge, too. Gentlemen like the duke do not simply act flirtatiously towards spinsters and women of your age and station out of *charity*, regardless of what that woman tried to tell you."

"He is not flirting with me, Mama."

"No, but he is singling you out. Here is my opinion on the matter, from what I have observed. The duke enjoys your company. You are clever, outspoken, confident, and you are pretty. You don't flirt with *him*, and you do not appear to be endeavouring to win his affections. It is refreshing for a man like that. So, as I said before, he enjoys your company. You are friends. It is a very small step from friendship to love, let me tell you. The two can be almost indistinguishable. There is no reason why you should *not* catch the duke, and Miss Bainbridge knows it."

Lavinia bit her lip.

Stop it! she wanted to scream. *Stop building up my hopes! He's not going to marry me, even if I wanted him to.*

I don't, of course. That would be nothing but foolishness. He's going to marry Miss Bainbridge, everybody knows it. Miss Bainbridge, or at least a woman just like her. Not somebody like me.

"I don't want to win his affections, Mama," she said at last. "He shall engage into matrimony with somebody more suitable, after all. There is little merit in indulging hope, is there not?"

Lady Brennon was quiet for a long moment.

"Did you hear of the Dowager's story, my dear?"

"What? No."

"She was madly in love with the old duke – his Grace's father – but he only married her for her money and her breeding. Because she would make a good duchess, you know. It is most distressing to witness a marriage decay in such a manner, when one party is full of affection and the other has yet to experience a single sentiment of it." Everybody in London knew how the old Duke treated his wife, and how she adored him all the way through it. She still does, as far as I know."

Lavinia glanced across the room to where the Dowager Duchess sat, surrounded by a cluster of friends, talking and laughing. There was a sort of hollowness in her face, even when she was smiling. A blankness behind the eyes, perhaps. Lavinia felt, not for the first time, a powerful pang of sympathy for the woman.

She didn't deserve that. Nobody deserves that.

"That's awful," Lavinia said, voice barely louder than a whisper. "The poor woman."

"Yes, I thought so. But it seems to me that the current duke – all of the Willenshire children, as a matter of fact – are keen not to make the mistakes of their parents. They've all married for love, if rumours are to be believed, and having seen them together, I quite agree. Why should the duke not marry for love, too?"

"But..."

"Do you think he loves Miss Bainbridge? Do you think *she* loves *him*?"

Lavinia shook her head. "No, but it's more complicated than that. It must be."

Lady Brennon only smiled faintly. "My darling girl, it is not as complicated as you think. Not nearly as complicated. Why not give it a try? Attempt to garner the duke's attention and observe the outcome. Miss Bainbridge wouldn't have warned you off if she hadn't seen you as a threat, would she?"

Lavinia had to grin at that. "No, she wouldn't, would she? That's quite an interesting point, Mama. And... and thank you. For standing up for me the way you did."

Lady Brennon winked, reaching out to pat Lavinia's cheek. "I do love my girls, Lavinia. I might not be the best mother in the country, but I love my girls."

There was no time for anything else, because at that moment, the door opened and the gentlemen began to file in, talking and laughing.

Lavinia found herself seeking out the duke and loathed the way her heart clenched when she saw him.

Stop it, she scolded. *You mustn't.*

Miss Bainbridge was across the room in an instant, all but glueing herself to the duke's side. She laughed and tossed her hair, smiling up into his face, and if she didn't *quite* smile smugly across the room at Lavinia, the intention was there.

Lavinia got up abruptly. "I'm tired, Mama, and so is Gillian. I'm going to retire for the night, and I'm taking her with me."

Lady Brennon sat back, folding her hands across her stomach.

"As you wish, my dear, as you wish. But do give heed to my words, if you would."

I could scarcely refrain from contemplating it, Lavinia reflected with a twinge of irritation.

Chapter Thirteen

"They call it Bath's Vauxhall Gardens," Mary announced, beaming over her shoulder. "I imagine it's rather spectacular. I cannot believe that we have never visited. Should we have gone at night, Alex, do you think?"

"I don't think it's *quite* the same as Vauxhall, Mama," Alexander said gently. "We can always go again, if we like the place."

The dowager shook her head. "No, I think not. It's not seemly to enjoy things too much, you know."

William caught Katherine's eye across the breakfast table and said nothing.

He had retired early to bed the previous night, mostly to escape Miss Bainbridge's determined attentions. It had been almost frightening – she drove everybody away, keeping him to herself and chained up with politeness. Frightening and noticeable. Her parents had watched blandly, and he knew that others would have noticed, too.

I won't be entrapped, he thought, with a rush of anger.

The Bainbridges were not down yet, but of course they would be accompanying the party to Sydney Gardens. The Brookford sisters were not down yet, either. He couldn't help noticing that Miss Lavinia Brookford had retreated from the drawing room almost immediately after he arrived, taking her younger sister with her. Katherine had told him later that Miss Gillian seemed rather tired and pale, and Miss Lavinia was clearly worried about her sister.

And yet, here I am, selfishly wishing she had stayed down to talk to me, he thought wryly, shaking his head at his own thoughtlessness. The locket sat in his pocket again, the familiar contours of the smooth oval warm under the pad of his thumb.

It hardly mattered, though. More and more, William began to feel that nothing mattered at all – not his choice of bride, not the inheritance he had to earn, not the fact he had kept the horse that killed his father. How *could* any of it matter?

Still, he had to admit, he was glad that the Brookford girls were definitely coming to Sydney Gardens.

I won't talk to her, though. It's a bad idea to converse too much with a woman when I intend to marry another. I will stick with Miss Bainbridge, or better yet, with Katherine.

"I thought it might be fun to divide into groups," Katherine said, innocently sipping her tea. "So that we can spend time with people outside of our cliches. William, Miss Lavinia will be your personal responsibility today."

William froze. "I beg your pardon?"

Surely she could not mean it. Not after he had confided in her about the secret betrothal. But then, it *was* Katherine.

Katherine drained her cup. "I think you heard me perfectly well."

***

Sydney Gardens was buzzing with activity. It was a splendid, sunlit day, and the denizens had assembled in great numbers in the Gardens.

The Willenshires had never attended the Gardens, just like they had never attended Vauxhall in London. That is, until the old Duke died. He hadn't approved of pleasure gardens. William could hear his sour, grating voice even now: *waste of money and waste of time.*

Katherine clapped her hands for attention, and the guests milled around her. They were at the entrance to the Gardens, and already people were craning their necks eagerly to look beyond the gates.

There was plenty to do – croquet, archery, fortune-tellers, clockwork displays, and more. William could see countless lanterns hanging over the Gardens, which of course wouldn't be seen in the daylight.

Perhaps we could come back at night, he thought, *and see the lights, bright enough to drown out the stars.*

There were refreshment stalls, as was to be expected, in the vicinity where they intended to partake of tea in due course. Most of the party had already resolved to indulge in the region's famed delicacies, and William found himself inclined to partake as well.

"To make things a little more interesting," Katherine was saying, her voice carrying easily across the crowd, "and to force us all to make new friends, we shall be pairing up and travelling in groups. This is so that nobody gets lost – I know many of us are not native to Bath, and if anyone has a sense of direction as bad as mine, I doubt that they shall make it home again."

There was a polite ripple of laughter at this. Katherine withdrew a list and began to read it.

He saw Miss Bainbridge flinch and then flush with anger when she learned that she was paired with a middle-aged gentleman. The anger cooled to white fury when Katherine announced that William and Miss Lavinia Brookford would accompany each other.

A hand shot up in the crowd. Mrs. Bainbridge's, William noticed.

"I am not sure I like this pairing-off business," the woman said stoutly. "I wish to walk with my husband."

"As you like," Katherine answered blandly. "But I think the rest of us are enjoying the idea."

Mrs. Bainbridge did not look pleased at this development. A quick glance around the crowd showed that most people were pleased with their partners, talking and laughing and planning out where they would go and when. Katherine had not chosen the partners at random – she had chosen wisely.

William glanced around, and found Miss Brookford standing near his elbow, eyeing him cautiously.

"Do you mind us being paired together?" she said at last. "I should hate for you to feel uncomfortable."

He smiled. "I'm not uncomfortable. I'm afraid I'm very dull, though. I just wanted to walk through the Gardens and take in the scenery."

She relaxed a little. "I would like that, too."

The company began to disperse, individuals pairing off in twos and fours as they made their way into the Gardens, engaging in lively conversation and merriment.

William saw that Lady Brennon was paired with his mother, and he relaxed a little more.

I am glad that my mother is having a good time, he thought. *She deserves it.*

For a few moments, he and Miss Brookford walked side by side in silence.

"We have two hours before we need to meet with the rest of the people," he said after a while. "Katherine has arranged tea, I think."

"Oh, yes, I want to try one of those famous buns. I've never had one, you know, and everybody admits that they are delicious."

"The Sally Lunns? Oh, yes, they're very tasty. Very sweet, if you like that sort of thing."

"I *adore* sweet things," Miss Brookford laughed. She flashed her dimples up at him, and William was struck anew by the wave of warm affection that rushed through his chest. He swallowed hard, directing his gaze to the road ahead of them.

The original, wide path that started at the gate gradually grew thinner, splintering off into countless crossroads and off-shoots, all well signposted. In places, he could see that, come the darkness, there would be performers there, likely the same sort of performers found in London's Vauxhall Gardens. Fire eaters, jugglers, tightrope walkers, people with rare and unique animals – monkeys, parrots, snakes, and even a tarantula in a cage once.

A little further along, he saw the looming shape of the place they were to have tea and confectioneries, with supper-boxes set at intervals here and there. He hoped that Katherine had organized a supper-box, rather than them taking tea inside. It was a fine day, fine enough to eat and drink out of doors.

Forgetting where he was and who he was with for just a moment, William turned his face up to the blue sky above him, tilting his head right back and closing his eyes. The gentle breeze felt luxurious on his skin, and the sun warmed his face, glowing pinkly through his closed eyelids.

When he finally opened his eyes, blinking in the light, and glanced down, he found that Miss Brookford was staring at him thoughtfully, her expression a little uncertain.

She flushed at once, clearly embarrassed to be caught staring and directed her gaze away. William felt heat rising to his face, too.

What was I thinking? What is it about this woman that makes me act so strangely?

"I don't believe I ever offered you an apology," he said after a pause.

She glanced up at him. "An apology?"

"Yes. When we first met – when we *truly* first met, I mean – I should have left the balcony at once. It was more proper. Instead, I stayed and talked with you."

"I didn't mind."

"I know, but a true gentleman would have left you at once."

She smiled wryly. "And a true lady would never have stepped onto the balcony at all. I think at the least we are as bad as each other."

He had to smile at that. "I cannot argue with that."

"And... frankly, I think I thought I had rather shocked you on our first meeting," she sighed, shaking her head. "I speak my mind more often than I should, I know."

"I think that if more people spoke their minds, the world would be a better place."

She chuckled. "I know a great many stalwarts of Society who would disagree."

"They can disagree all they like. The world is changing."

She shot another glance up at him. "Indeed it is."

They walked on in silence for a few more minutes. It was a comfortable silence, not the awkward absence of conversation, and William felt himself relaxing more and more. They passed a few people from their party, clustered together in a group of six, all of them laughing and talking. William realized that without planning it, they were heading towards the tea-house.

He wasn't sure he was pleased about this. Once they reached it, he would feel obliged to go in and meet the others, then their private conversation would end.

"How does your sister fare, if I may inquire? I was disappointed to hear that she wouldn't be joining us."

Miss Brookford sighed. "Gillian is simply fatigued, that is all. She requires a period of repose, yet Mama does not permit her to rest until it is far too late, and by then, she is too wearied to undertake any task. I was going to stay with her, but Mama and Gillian insisted that I come out. Truly, siblings cause the most anxiety out of anything else in the world."

He laughed aloud at that and then blinked, surprised at himself.

"I have to agree," he said at last, aware that Miss Brookford was eyeing him with a smile. "My own siblings are a constant cause of stress. Thank heavens they are all married. Of course, Alexander was always Mother's favourite. I suppose I was Father's favourite, although I'm not sure that is much of a compliment."

He bit his lip, glancing away.

Too much, William, he scolded himself. *You shouldn't have said that.*

A quick glance at Miss Brookford showed that she was staring down at the ground, brow furrowed.

"I know what you mean," she said suddenly, giving a loose shrug. "I worry a great deal about Gillian. Is it selfish, do you suppose, to worry about myself, too? After all, what will I do when she's gone?"

"I believe it's perfectly natural. At least with only the two of you, your parents would not play favourites."

She gave a bark of laughter, and William realized that he had mis-stepped.

"I wish that were true. I love my family, honestly, I do, but it's clear that Gillian is Mama's favourite, at the very least. She does not hide that. Oh, it isn't that she's unkind or cruel, but... well, Gillian is the sweet, pretty one, the one who wants to marry and start a family, and it seems that our hopes all hang upon her."

"You do yourself a disservice, Miss Brookford."

She drew in a deep breath, squaring her shoulders, and a sort of mask seemed to come down over her face. William only realized just how open and vulnerable her expression had truly been when it disappeared.

"On the contrary. I am not looking for compliments, your Grace. I am only being honest. I think that honesty is a rather fine quality, don't you think?"

"It is."

"I strive to show it in my life. Unfortunately, it seems that honesty isn't valued in ladies — at least, not *true* honesty."

"I'm inclined to agree. My sister, Katherine, has always been rather forthright, and often criticised for it."

"She's remarkably kind, I must say. She has taken pains to make my sister and me welcome," Miss Brookford breathed in deeply, gaze fixed straight ahead.

William found his own gaze glued to her profile. His heart thudded in his chest.

I don't want to talk about Katherine, or Miss Gillian, or our parents. I want to talk about you.

"Do you have much family beyond your siblings?" Miss Brookford asked abruptly, flashing him a tired smile. It was a fairly ordinary question, one edging more towards Polite Conversation territory, as opposed to their too-frank discussion of before.

"We have some family on our father's side," William managed at last. "Cousins, aunts, uncles, and so on. We... we were never close to them. My father, it seems, rather cut off any kind of communication with his family. I often wonder if they saw something cruel in him and distanced themselves accordingly. Of course, we had no such opportunity."

She glanced sharply at him. It occurred to William, not for the first time, that he should not speak so freely about his father's cruelty. It should be ignored, swept under the rug and tactfully forgotten about.

No. Why should I cover over his sins? He was a vile man, and he made us suffer. Why should the world not know about it?

He opened his mouth, not entirely sure what he intended to say, but Miss Brookford spoke first.

"The Bainbridges are coming our way," she said, nodding down the path ahead.

Disappointment and frustration flooded through William in equal measure. He glanced forward, and saw that Miss Brookford was indeed right. The three Bainbridges, who had apparently all ignored their assigned partners and stuck together in a trio, were heading purposefully to the path towards them. Miss Bainbridge led the way, a look of determination on her face, and William just knew that she would glue herself to his side and refuse to let him go.

He was a little surprised at the annoyance he felt. He did not *want* to talk to Miss Bainbridge. He wanted to talk to Miss Brookford, alone, about subjects that were never touched on in polite Society.

I want to kiss her.

Stop it!

"You are going to marry her, aren't you?" Miss Brookford said suddenly, earning herself a shocked stare from William.

"That's... that's hardly proper for us to discuss," he managed at last.

Miss Brookford shrugged. "She would make a fine duchess."

"Well, yes," he managed lamely, "but that's not all one should consider in a spouse."

"No, I suppose not. Forgive me, your Grace. I... I am not feeling well. I shouldn't speak this way."

He swallowed hard, glancing down at her again. The Bainbridges were nearly upon them, and then of course all conversation would stop.

"Please, Miss Brookford. Don't apologise for honesty. Never apologise for it. Not to me, at any rate."

And you are right, Miss Brookford. I am going to marry her. I have to marry her. She would never let me out of the engagement, not when she has me exactly where she wants me.

She glanced up at him and gave a slow smile. "That means a great deal, your Grace."

And then Miss Bainbridge reached them, face flushed from fast walking.

"What a surprise," she wheezed. "Fancy stumbling upon you both here."

Chapter Fourteen

Miss Bainbridge cornered the duke, as Lavinia had known she would. Anyway, they were almost at the tea-house.

Streams of people were approaching their meeting point, not just from their own party, but others, too. People talked and laughed and gestured, some hurrying towards the confectioneries, keen to eat. Lavinia found herself walking alone.

Miss Bainbridge, having slid her arm through the duke's, hurried him ahead, so that it was just the two of them. Lavinia was left to fall behind, walking with Mr. and Mrs. Bainbridge. Of course, *they* did not care to talk to her. They tossed their heads, bestowing frosty smiles on her, and talked quietly among themselves, excluding her from the conversation.

She tried not to care.

He's a duke, she reminded herself. *He's not some nervous, gawky young man. If he wanted to talk to me, well, then, he would. He would. And he isn't.*

This was a more painful thought than she'd anticipated. Ducking her head, Lavinia concentrated instead on the paving stones beneath her feet.

At least heartbreak – if that is what this is, of which I'm not convinced – is not doing anything to my appetite. I'm absolutely starving.

On that note, somebody cleared their throat beside her. She glanced up to find a short, round-faced young man with round spectacles smiling hopefully at her.

"Miss, er, Miss Brookford, isn't it?"

"Lord Langley," she said, a little pleased at herself for remembering. Lord Ethan Langley was a single man with a half-decent title and a good fortune, with two left feet when it came to dancing and a surprising passion for music. He was about three and twenty, not particularly handsome, and had shown a great deal of interest in Gillian.

Lady Brennon wanted Gillian to look for "larger prizes", as she put it, and there were certainly wealthier men than Lord Langley in the party.

There were poorer men, too, which Lavinia had pointed out. Besides, Gillian's face brightened whenever she saw Lord Langley, and the pair of them had talked about music and literature and all sorts of frivolities for hours on end at previous gatherings.

"I see that Miss Gillian is not here today," Lord Langley said, falling into step beside Lavinia.

At least I don't have to face the humiliation of having nobody to escort me into the tea-house, Lavinia thought, biting back a mirthless smile.

"Yes, she's rather ill, I'm afraid."

"Oh, I am sorry. Is it serious? Should a physician be fetched? I could fetch one at once, Miss Brookford, if necessary."

She gave a more sincere smile at that. "No, thank you, Lord Langley. It is kind of you, though. No, my sister is just tired. It's nothing a little rest won't settle. I daresay you'll see her at dinner tonight. She was disappointed to miss out on the Gardens, though. Too much dancing, I think."

Lord Langley nodded seriously. "Dancing is a very pleasant pastime, I'm sure, but dreadfully tiring. Only yesterday, Miss Gillian said..."

He launched into an account of some conversation that he and Gillian had shared. Lavinia smiled politely, but her mind drifted.

The duke and Miss Bainbridge had, by this time, disappeared into the crowd. She had no doubt that she would not see them again.

***

"He's fond of you, that is certain."

Lavinia glanced up, meeting her mother's eye. "What do you mean?"

They were heading back to the house, just the two of them rattling around in their carriage. Lady Brennon sat opposite, her feet propped up on the other carriage seat, smiling to herself, looking pleased.

"I am talking about the duke, of course," Lady Brennon shook her head. "You are so naive. Who else? He was so pleased to be paired with you, anybody could see that."

"He's a polite man, Mama. If he were dismayed, he'd never let on."

"Perhaps, perhaps. But I saw how his face lit up. I saw the way his eyes tracked you around."

Lavinia bit her lower lip, hard.

I wish I could believe that.

"Of course," Lady Brennon continued, half speaking to herself now, "A man like him has a great deal more to consider than his own personal preferences. He may *like* you, but he must consider a great deal when it comes to choosing the next duchess. This is when it would serve you, my dear, to be more *ladylike*. Do you understand what I mean?"

"Perfectly, Mama. Still, I don't intend to change myself to suit some man's idea of what a bride should be."

Lady Brennon sniffed. "And that is why you're on the cusp of spinsterhood, my dear. It's of no matter. I believe you might be right about that Bainbridge girl. She has her eye on him, and she *would* make a perfect duchess, anyone can see that. Your manners are *not* what they should be. Oh, I do wish he'd settled his eye on Gillian. She's a little young, true, but perhaps..." Lady Brennon faltered, glancing over at her daughter for the first time since she'd begun speaking.

Lavinia tried to compose her expression, not entirely sure what her mother was seeing in her face. Whatever she saw, it wasn't good.

"Oh, my dear," Lady Brennon breathed. "You like him, don't you?"

Lavinia pressed her lips together in a thin line. "He's a nice enough man. He's pleasant. Of course I like him."

"That," Lady Brennon said firmly, "was not what I meant."

Yes, Mama, I know what you meant. I do not wish to discuss it. Is that so wrong?

Lavinia wanted to scream, and cry, and drum her feet on the seat like a child, and shout that it was not *fair* that she should finally, *finally* meet a man that made her heart beat fast, a man she wanted to speak to, wanted to be near, wanted to *marry*, only to have him whipped out from under her nose by a Miss Bainbridge.

She wanted to do all of that, but of course she did not. It wasn't proper, and would do no good, at the end of the day. Besides, Lavinia wasn't entirely sure she wanted to manage her mother's well-meaning sympathy. Perhaps saying it aloud would make it more real than it ought to be.

"Weren't you the one who told me to manage my feelings, Mama?" Lavinia said, flashing a wry smile. "You gave Gillian the same advice. You told her not to feel *too much* until she was sure of a return, so that the feelings might not be wasted. I thought it was rather good advice."

Lady Brennon started to look a little unsure.

There, you see, Lavinia thought. *I can be as cool and composed as I please. You taught me that, at least.*

"Well, I suppose so," Lady Brennon said at last. "That is a fair point. You *might secure his feelings* still, you know. If you were to apply yourself. Mightn't you, Lavinia?"

Lavinia smiled faintly, glancing out of the window. The white streets of Bath zipped past, one after the other.

"Yes," she said, guardedly. "I might."

It was easy enough to evade Lady Brennon once they returned home. The house was chaos, with everybody trying to get up to their bedchambers to change, some wanting refreshments, some wanting to sit down, everybody wanting *something*. The long-suffering servants darted here and there, trying to take care of everyone. The Dowager Duchess glided amongst it all, the very image of a gracious host. Lavinia could not see the duke, and she was glad of that.

Once she returned to her bedchamber, Lavinia changed into a plain gown and sturdy boots. She took the back stairs – shocking, yes, but she was lucky enough not to encounter any disapproving servants and slipped out into the courtyard without incident.

I should have brought a maid, Lavinia thought wryly, and struck out towards the stables at once.

Naturally, the stables had been off-limits to her since they had arrived. Lady Brennon had been very clear on that. Ladies might ride, occasionally, with gentlemen, but they did *not* frequent stables. Stables were dirty, smelly, crowded, and the province of men.

And since this entire excursion was for Gillian's benefit, and Gillian would not be benefited by being seen with a sister stinking of horse and covered in straw, Lavinia obeyed.

Today was the last straw, however.

Lavinia stuck her head into the stables, intending to make her way down the rows of stalls and inspecting the horses inside. She'd seen some of the horses the other guests had brought, and they *were* marvellous creatures. A hunting party had been planned for later in the week, and that would take up just about every horse in the stables. Lavinia was looking forward for the opportunity to ride. And if she chose to take a little practice run earlier, well, what of it? Her father had agreed on bringing Stepper along and so she thought that her favourite horse could do with the exercise, and so could she.

She was about to enter the stables when something caught her eye outside.

Frowning, Lavinia rounded the building, squinting at a paddock set alongside.

The paddock was empty, with the exception of one horse. Immediately, she remembered the fabulous stallion she'd seen on the way here, with the glossy black mane and the beautifully arched neck.

Sorry, Stepper, she thought with a wry smile. *I'll come back to see you soon, I promise.*

Leaving the stables behind, Lavinia moved towards the paddock. She stepped up onto the lowest slat of the fence, which allowed her to rest her arms on the top of the fence, and just watched.

The creature was running round and round in circles, tossing its head. Its mane was sleek and glossy, rippling out behind it. In places, its black coat appeared almost blue, glistening and shimmering. She imagined that somebody had brushed the horse's coat till it gleamed.

The horse paused in its galloping, tossing its head towards her. Large, dark eyes lingered on her, gleaming with intelligence. The horse was watching her, she realized.

After a moment, the horse began to troop towards her, head bobbing, eyes cautious.

Thankfully, Lavinia had planned to bring treats for the horses, and her pockets were full of sliced carrots. She withdrew one piece, holding it out carefully.

The horse paused just out of arm's reach, watching her guardedly. Up close, he was even larger than she had thought. She could get up on Stepper's back without a mounting block, if necessary, but not up onto this horse. He was *huge*.

She kept her hand steady, waiting. Horses could be skittish things, for all their size, and this particular one seemed more skittish than most.

Lavinia held her breath. After what seemed like an eternity, the horse leaned forward a few more inches, and gently picked up the piece of carrot from her palm, soft mouth lipping at her skin.

He crunched his treat, eyeing her thoughtfully. Lavinia allowed herself a small smile of triumph. She reached out to touch the horse's nose, but he flicked his head back, ears pressing against his head, and she took the hint. Instead, she reached into her pocket for more carrots.

The horse crunched happily, coming a few steps closer. The next time that Lavinia reached out to touch his soft nose, his ears only flickered a little. He allowed it, and her heart leapt.

"Aren't you beautiful?" she murmured.

The horse whinnied gently.

And then a man's voice, frantic with fear, cut through the silence. The stallion's ears flattened against his head again.

"What on earth are you doing, you foolish girl? Whatever you do, don't touch that horse! *Don't touch that horse!*"

Chapter Fifteen

It seemed today that William's study was not the comforting haven it generally was.

In fact, he found the silence and order a little grating.

The idyllic blue skies from earlier had faded away, replaced by heavy, bruised-grey clouds, hanging low and threatening rain. There was a great deal of talk about if the weather was about to take a turn, and what could be done about the planning of a hunting excursion and upcoming picnic if it did.

Frankly, William could not have cared less. He was thoroughly sick of smiling and mincing around his mother's guests, hearing the same platitudes repeated over and over again, not a stitch of meaning in any of them.

"Goodness, look at those clouds! Shall we have rain do you think?"

"We are lucky the weather held for our trip through the Park. Don't you think so, your Grace?"

"I hope the rain will not ruin our picnic."

And so on. He'd heard all of the comments, over and over again. Mostly they had come from Miss Bainbridge.

Oh, that wretched girl. William was beginning to feel distinctly ungentlemanly towards her. Her forthrightness and cool, steady logic, which he'd so admired in the early stages of their acquaintance, had been swept away and replaced with nonsense and smooth Society manners. He knew the cause.

She's no longer certain of me, he thought, biting his lip. *Even with the agreement between us. Confident as she is, she sees Miss Brookford as a threat and thinks that she must now work hard to secure me. I'm not a sure affair anymore.*

Indeed, that was nonsense. Miss Brookford *had* been pleasant to him, that was for sure, but that meant nothing. But Miss Bainbridge clearly believed it and acted accordingly.

What sort of man must I be, to make my betrothed feel so insecure? I agreed to the match, and there will be no turning back.

It had taken him a full hour to shake her off once he returned home. What on earth would things be like once they were married?

A tap on the door made him jump. William cleared his throat, trying to compose himself.

None of the work on his desk had been looked at, of course. Soon he would have to think about dressing for dinner. How could a whole afternoon slip away?

"Who is it?"

"Only me, your Grace," came the butler's familiar voice. "I have brought tea."

"Oh, excellent. Thank you."

The butler came in, carrying the tea-things on a highly polished silver tray, bright enough to hurt William's eyes. He wished, not for the first time, that not *everything* around him had to be polished to a shine, cleaned and scrubbed and shined until it gleamed.

"I thought I should tell you, your Grace, that one of the young lady guests has been seen heading towards the stables," the butler said, disapproval heavy in his voice. "Her Grace, the Dowager Duchess, remarked upon it. Shall I fetch her back? I am not sure she was chaperoned, your Grace."

"I'm sure she won't come to harm in the stables."

The butler made a little sound. "That is hardly the point, your Grace."

"Do tell me you aren't one of those chaps who think ladies can't be interested in horses," William remarked, lifting an eyebrow. The butler said nothing, only poured out a cup of tea. William took a sip. He *was* hungry. He'd barely touched his bun, despite the rest of their guests digging in eagerly. Frankly, he found the confectioneries too sweet.

The butler straightened, hesitating. There was clearly more.

"It's just that..."

"What?" William asked, taking another sip of too-hot tea. He was getting a headache. "What's the matter?"

"It's just that a particular horse is out in the paddocks, your Grace. The lady might see it."

"What does that matter?"

The butler pressed his lips together. "A *particular* horse, your Grace."

There was a heartbeat of time before William understood. When he did, a wave of panic flooded through him.

What if that creature hurts someone else? People will wonder why I let it live after it threw my father, or why I didn't at least give it away.

I won't have a suitable answer.

He flew over to the window, through which he could see the fields behind the house, as well as the stable block and the paddocks around it.

And there, quite clearly, without the slightest mistake of what it could be, he saw that wretched black stallion in the paddock closest to the stables.

A lady had half-climbed up the fence, and was leaning over, holding out a hand. There appeared to be something in her palm. As he was watching, horrified, the stallion delicately took the treat, nose snuffling at her hand, as demure as anything.

"I thought I made it clear that horse was meant to be kept away," William said, voice wobbling. "Imagine if one of the guests chose to ride it, or believed it was a suitable mount for the hunting party, of all things."

The butler cleared his throat. "Yes, your Grace. I am not sure why the horse would be in the paddock, but the grooms insist that the horse requires exercise and fresh air. They say the creature is tamer than it once was."

"That'll count for nothing, if Society finds out that I kept the horse that killed my father!"

William could hear his voice pitching, childishly hysterical. He squeezed his eyes closed, biting his lower lip hard.

It doesn't matter. Just send somebody out to bring her back, put the horse back in the stables, and have a word with her mamma. The girl really shouldn't be out unchaperoned at a party so full of gentlemen, it's generally not very...

His thoughts cut off abruptly when the lady turned around, glancing back towards the house as if her attention was caught by something, hand lifted to prevent her bonnet from flying off her head.

It was, of course, Miss Lavinia Brookford.

William felt that he ought to have guessed that right away. Naturally, only a lady like Miss Brookford would go out alone to investigate the stables, only to find what was likely the only man-killing horse in Bath.

William acted before he knew what he was doing. Wrenching open the window, he stuck out his head, the cool air taking his breath away after the stuffiness of the study.

"What on earth are you doing, you foolish girl? Whatever you do, don't touch that horse! *Don't touch that horse!*"

Perhaps, in hindsight, it was not the most polite thing to shout. The butler drew in a sharp, surprised breath, but William could not have cared less.

She'd heard him, he *knew* she'd heard him, but she only stared blankly at the house, baffled, clearly with no idea who was shouting at her and why.

Biting back a curse, William withdrew back into the study.

"I will deal with this," he told the butler shortly, and then broke into a run.

He managed to race through the house without being seen, except by some baffled footmen. William shot out into the cool air, realizing to his chagrin that he had left his jacket up in his study, and was in fact in his shirtsleeves.

It was too late now to do anything about it, of course. Clenching his teeth, he ran faster, crossing the courtyard.

He could now see the stables up ahead, with the paddock to one side. Miss Brookford was still perched up on the fence, her back to him. The horse was close enough to her now that it could nudge her shoulder with its nose, which it did when she did not produce another piece of carrot quickly enough.

In his mind's eye, he saw the horse bucking, his father flying forward out of the saddle. He saw the widening of the old duke's eyes, the first glimmer of fear that William had ever seen on his father's face.

What sort of creature could make a man like *that* feel afraid?

"Miss Brookford!" he bellowed. "*Miss Brookford!*"

She turned to look at him, aghast, as any woman would when confronted with a madman running at full speed towards her. It occurred to him briefly that he had to look like an absolute sight, in his shirtsleeves, hair a mess, eyes wild, racing towards her, yelling.

"Your Grace?" she managed, dropping down from the fence. "What on earth is the matter?"

The horse put back its ears and huffed, jerking its head up and down. What did that mean? William had never liked horses, even before the incident, and he had no idea what those movements were supposed to mean. He supposed that the horse was upset. Somebody had once said that when horses put back their ears, it meant they were angry.

Panic spiked in his chest.

"Get away, you simpleton! Get away!"

Miss Brookford began to look wary instead of confused. William's lungs were on fire. He skidded to a halt, gripping Miss Brookford's shoulders and hauling her bodily away from the fence.

The horse snorted again, lowering its head like a bull about to charge. William tried to drag the woman further away, but she struggled, attempting to yank her arm free from his grip.

"William, what are you *doing*?" she gasped.

She succeeded in pulling her arm free, only to lose her balance, slipping on the uneven ground. She would have fallen heavily if William had not snatched desperately at her, winding one arm around her waist and pulling her close with a *thud* that knocked the breath out of both of their bodies.

Then clarity seemed to trickle in, and it occurred to William just how much of a raving fool he had been. And, of course, that he now had his arm *around a woman's waist* and was holding her close.

He released her at once. She stepped back, red-faced, and drew in a deep, fortifying breath.

"What," she said carefully, "are you doing, your Grace? Have you gone mad? You are acting as if you are."

She called me William.

The thought came from nowhere, burrowing its way through William's head and making a home at the front of his mind. He swallowed hard. No doubt her slip-up was due to surprise, or perhaps stress. He could hardly complain about her informality when he had come rushing towards her at full speed, yelling like a fool.

"My apologies," he said, breathless, "but I saw you feeding that horse from my study window."

"Are you the one who called me a foolish girl?" Miss Brookford asked at once, eyebrows lifting.

He flushed. "I... I did not think. I just reacted... I hope you can forgive me."

She held his gaze for a long moment, then sighed, shaking her head. "You're our host. I suppose I must forgive you."

"That's not the case at all, Miss Brookford. I should never have... I did not mean to... oh, heavens. I'm making a mess of this. The thing is, that horse is dangerous. Quite dangerous. You shouldn't go near it. Did none of the grooms tell you?"

She shrugged. "I didn't see a groom. I didn't see anyone. I came to find my horse, Stepper, but I saw this beautiful creature, and I thought... oh, he can't be dangerous. He's as sweet as anything. Didn't you see him taking carrots from my hand? He was so gentle."

William bit his lip. "Miss Brookford, you have no idea of the danger."

"Tell me, then. What is the danger?"

He missed a beat. "None of your concern."

"*None of my concern?*" Miss Brookford repeated, folding her arms tight across her chest. "You shout at me from a window, come racing out like a madman in your shirtsleeves – my mother would have an apoplexy if she saw you talking to me now, by the way – and then you grab me and all but tackle me to the ground. You ramble on about danger but do not offer any explanations. And you tell me it's none of my concern? I beg to differ, your Grace."

William bit his lip. Perhaps it was his imagination, but it seemed that the horse was looking at him critically, too.

Perhaps I deserve it.

He closed his eyes briefly. "The situation is complicated, Miss Brookford."

She narrowed her eyes. "Is that so? I'm sure a clever man like you can summarise it. Do try and explain."

William drew in a deep, shaky breath. He found his gaze drawn over Miss Brookford's shoulder to where the horse stood, entirely still, dark eyes fixed on him.

"That horse killed my father, Miss Brookford."

There was a long, taut silence after that. Miss Brookford blinked up at him, disbelief, horror, and understanding crossing her face in rapid succession.

"Oh," she said at last, voice small. "Oh, I did not... I didn't know that."

William smiled wryly. "So you see what I mean when I say that the horse is dangerous, Miss Brookford. He had not been ridden much before my father bought him, and not at all afterwards. He might harm you, and I should be responsible for that."

She swallowed. "I had no idea, your Grace. Truly. I..." she trailed off, her gaze darting over his shoulder. He turned to see the butler huffing and puffing his way towards them, clutching one of William's jackets.

He bit back a smile.

"Your jacket, your Grace," the butler gasped, as soon as he was close enough to be heard. "It is entirely too cold, and not... not proper for you to be out of doors without it."

The man's meaning was plain, even without the pointed look he shot at Miss Brookford.

Grimacing, William took the jacket and slid it on. "Thank you."

"Shall I escort Miss Brookford back to the house?"

William glanced at her, waiting for her to answer. Miss Brookford met his gaze and held it, the instant seeming to drag out forever before she spoke.

"No, thank you," she said at last. "I can find my way back."

The butler pursed his lips, glancing at William for confirmation. He gave a short nod, and the butler barely repressed a sigh, turning and heading back towards the house.

At that moment, the horse seemed to take offence at the butler's tone, giving a sharp whinny and half rearing up onto its back hooves.

William gave a yelp of fear before he could stop himself, backing away at once.

"It's alright, your Grace," Miss Brookford said at once, laying a hand on his arm. It was as if she were trying to soothe him, rather than the horse. "This fellow is just a little uncertain around new people. You said he had not been ridden much?"

William swallowed hard, shaking his head. "No. Not at all. He... he has never been aggressive towards anyone else. He doesn't bite, or kick, although I can't help but worry that he might. I am sorry, I should not have dragged you into all this. It's not your concern. I... I would be grateful if you didn't mention the horse. People may think I ought to have had him killed, after he threw my father."

Miss Brookford tilted her head. "I'm inclined to blame the rider, rather than the horse. I hope that doesn't offend you, by the way."

He allowed himself a small smile. "No, you would be right. My father... well, he believed that horses must be broken. He employed whips and spurs and so on, and he expected me to do the same. I... I have never been much good at horse riding. I never had a taste for it, even before..." he swallowed reflexively, eyeing the horse. "Certainly not after."

Miss Brookford nodded slowly, following his gaze. She took a careful step towards the fence, reaching out a hand to the horse. William stiffened, fighting back his urge to grab her and haul her back out of danger.

She laid her hand on the horse's nose. The creature only snorted, lipping at her fingers in hopes of more carrots. When it was clear that there were none, it only flicked its ears in disappointment.

"It's a sweet animal," she said quietly. "I bet I could ride this horse. I bet *you* could, your Grace. Horses like this don't allow themselves to be forced. One must *persuade*."

"I would rather die than ride that horse. Or any horse, for that matter."

She gave a chuckle at that. "Well, that really *is* none of my concern, I suppose. But riding is such excellent exercise, you know."

"I'm sure you are correct but I prefer to get my exercise elsewhere."

Seeing that there were no more carrots to be had, the horse gave another whinny, tossed his head, and turned to gallop back across the paddock, beginning a wide circuit of the field. His glossy mane rippled in the wind, and William felt a flash of guilt.

How often is this creature exercised? Did I ever bother to find out?

"I expect you're shocked that I kept the horse after it killed my father," he said aloud. "I haven't an excuse for you, if that's what you want to hear. I simply couldn't bear to get rid of it. It didn't seem fair."

She tilted her head, looking up at him. "I was thinking nothing of the sort. It's your business, and if your father was as cruel towards his horses as you say, I'm not surprised that one of them threw him."

William swallowed hard, watching the horse gallop. "It was meant to be me riding him, you know. I wouldn't, because I saw that the horse was nervy. It was more than that, though. I was afraid, frankly. I often wonder whether I would have died instead, if I'd gotten into that saddle."

"Perhaps you might have been hurt," she acknowledged. "But you are a very different man to your father. I think things would have been different."

He glanced sharply at her. "Some people think that I am very much like him."

She held his gaze. "I think differently. Do you *want* to be like him?"

"No!" the word was out, bitten off and angry, before William could stop himself. Miss Brookford did not flinch. She only nodded, as if he had confirmed something for her.

"There you are, then. I think you should ride again, if you want my opinion. We could ride together."

He swallowed. "Perhaps."

Distantly, the dressing gong rang in the house, a sign that it was time for the guests to prepare for dinner. Sighing, she turned as if to leave, but paused, glancing back.

"What is his name?"

"Hm?"

"The horse," she nodded at the creature still galloping around the field. "What is his name?"

"Oh. Do you know, I cannot remember? He must have had one, but I can't recall it. Perhaps you could name him."

He wasn't sure what made him add the last part, but it was worth it. Miss Brookford's face lit up.

"Can I?"

He nodded, smiling. "Take your time and choose a good one. Let me know what you have decided."

Still beaming, she turned and began to hurry across towards the house. William watched her go, his heart hammering against the inside of his ribcage.

A movement at one of the windows caught his eye, and he glanced up in time to see a figure shift out of view. A female figure, and he could guess who it was. A cold chill ran down his spine.

In all the excitement, he'd almost forgotten about his betrothal.

Don't be a fool, William. Don't. Miss Brookford is not for you.

He glanced over at the field and found that the horse had stopped dead in the middle of the paddock, and was staring at him. Reddening, William turned on his heel and hurried back towards the house.

Chapter Sixteen

Lavinia inspected her reflection, worrying her lower lip between her teeth.

Well, I never thought I'd start worrying over my clothes because of a man, she thought wryly.

She'd chosen a checked green muslin, not *entirely* suitable for a house party but quite good enough for a picnic. The day was fine, if a little overcast, and the promised rain had not arrived.

Spirits were high. People were looking forward to the picnic, Gillian most of all. Apparently, Lord Langley – who had been sitting next to her at supper the previous night, while Lavinia found herself sandwiched between a prim and disapproving widow and a middle-aged gentleman who mostly ignored her and slurped his soup – had asked Gillian to show him how to make daisy-chains. This had come on the heels of Gillian confessing herself an avid gardener. Personally, Lavinia was sure the man could have come up with something better than making *daisy chains*, but Gillian was charmed and excited, so that was that.

It was pleasant to see her sister enjoying herself so much. Lord Langley's attentions at supper had been marked, his disappointment at not seeing her at the Park most intense.

And once Gillian is gone, Lavinia thought, not for the first time, *It will be just Mama, Papa and me.*

That wasn't a particularly pleasant thought.

She tweaked anxiously at a curl, turning her figure this way and that, to make sure the gown still looked suitable. It was last year's gown – no, the year before – and the guests here were a remarkably fashionable crowd. Miss Bainbridge, for example, had not worn anything at all from last year's Season, if gossip was to be believed. Not even a pair of gloves or a bonnet. Her entire wardrobe was new.

And here we can barely afford rent on our London house, Lavinia thought grimly.

Lady Brennon came bustling in, resplendent in a white lawn dress, covered in embroidered flowers, and an old-fashioned straw bonnet.

"Well, well, Lavinia, not ready yet? Gillian has been ready for quite some time! They are all getting ready to leave. Shall we go?"

Lavinia took one last look at herself in the glass.

This is as good as it is going to get.

"Yes," she said mildly. "I'm ready."

***

The picnic was to be held on a hill behind the house, with beautiful views overlooking a valley, a large pond spread out below. Despite the heavy clouds overhead, it was fairly warm, and there was no danger of rain.

The guests trailed out of the house in twos and fours, talking and laughing. The servants had, of course, gone on ahead with the supplies and so on, with a few of the ladies bringing baskets with their own extra goodies and picnic blankets, for the joy of spreading their own blanket out.

Lady Brennon was one of those women. She strode along by the dowager's side, both deep in conversation. The Dowager Duchess was apparently too slight and weak to carry her own basket, so Lady Brennon carried them both with ease.

Lord Langley came and found Gillian very quickly, and they soon fell to the back of the group, with a cheerful, round-faced chaperone following along behind. Lavinia was left to walk alone.

She had spotted the duke at once. He walked with his brothers and sister, along with the in-laws. He kept his head down and seemed preoccupied. Miss Bainbridge had not yet fought her way to him.

Nothing ventured, nothing gained, Lavinia thought, drew in a breath, and sped up her pace. She fell into step beside the duke, who glanced briefly down at her with a guarded expression.

For some reason, Lavinia's heart sank.

"Good morning, your Grace," she said brightly. "Are you looking forward to the picnic?"

"I do not particularly enjoy eating out of doors," he answered hesitantly. "But I don't wish to spoil the atmosphere."

"I'm sure no one would think that."

He gave a tight smile and a bow, and then abruptly sped up his pace, soon leaving Lavinia behind.

She could have scurried after him, though, if she had had less self-respect. As it was, Lavinia stared at his retreating back for a moment, trying to work out what, exactly, had just happened.

He had snubbed her. No, it wasn't a *definite* snub, but it had been pointed. He had made a polite but brief reply, and then hurried away. He didn't *want* to talk to her.

Did I say something wrong? I thought that yesterday, we...

She pinched off the thought abruptly, swallowing hard. The truth was, she did not know *what* had happened between them the day before. She hadn't understood what was going on at all, until the man came haring out of the house, screaming and waving his arms like a madman. It might have been funny if she wasn't suddenly afraid he was going to do something awful, like throw her over the fence.

She could still feel his strong fingers on her shoulders, his arm around her waist. It had been clear from his face that he knew he had made a mistake, a breach of propriety.

Nobody had seen, though, for which Lavinia was thankful. No doubt she would have suffered the worst of it, being the lady in question, the one who had gone out to see *horses* of all things.

But their conversation afterwards had been... well, it felt almost as if she were seeing the real man behind the dukedom. It was thrilling. Lavinia had believed, truly believed, that things had changed between the duke and her. Perhaps a friendship might flourish, heaven knew she needed friends.

Perhaps it might become something more. Perhaps. It horrified her to feel her heart surging at this thought. Of *something more*. With *him*.

It was frustrating to be kept away from him at dinner, but Lavinia had managed it gracefully. She was sure she would have an opportunity to talk to him today, and she was right.

She had had the opportunity, but he had hurried away almost at once.

Glancing around, Lavinia was relieved to see that nobody else had seen it. Sighing, she applied herself to climbing the last stretch of their walk, up the hill towards the peak.

***

"Would you care for some currant jelly, your Grace?" Lavinia spoke up.

The duke flinched, as if he had not seen her at his elbow.

The blankets were all laid out, most people reclining with their friends. The food was being laid out, and some people were strolling between the blankets, clearly deciding where to sit.

The duke was one of those people, looking rather at a loss. Lavinia had risen to her feet and gone to stand beside him.

When he only stared blankly at her, she gestured to her picnic blanket, laden with goodies, currant jelly among them.

"You could join us," she offered.

He swallowed hard, avoiding her eye. "I... I think I ought to sit with my mother, Miss Brookford. But thank you for your offer. It was... it was very kind, and the currant jelly looks remarkably good. Thank you."

He made a stiff, awkward bow, and then hurried away, leaving Lavinia at a loss once again.

At least, he *made* to move away and would have done if she had not reached out and grabbed his sleeve.

Now *that* was a terrible breach of propriety, and she dropped her hand away at once. He had already stopped dead, face beet red.

"I beg your pardon," she said quietly, glancing around to make sure nobody else had noticed. "But I have done something to offend you, your Grace?"

His eyes fluttered shut, just for a moment. "No, nothing. I... Do excuse me."

She said nothing, letting him walk away this time. Lavinia watched him weave his way through the spread-out blankets, shoulders hunched and head down.

As he passed the Bainbridges' blanket – only the three of them sat there – Miss Bainbridge spoke to him. Of course she did. Lavinia could not hear what she said, but the inviting smile and tilted head said it all.

The duke hesitated, only for a moment, and then lowered himself to sit beside her on the blanket. Miss Bainbridge threw a quick, triumphant look over her shoulder, meeting Lavinia's eye squarely.

She turned away, crimson, and left Miss Bainbridge to her success, flopping down on the blanket again.

"What are you standing around for, dear?" Lady Brennon remarked, entirely engrossed by her cream biscuit. "Why don't you pour us all some tea?"

Lavinia poured the tea.

***

After the picnic, there were games of croquet and bowls, and even a few mild-mannered card games conducted between groups of people on their picnic blankets.

Lavinia did not join in. She sat on her blanket, staring into space, wishing she had an appetite for the dainties spread out before her.

Why the sudden change in attitude? She wondered, for the hundredth time. *What did I do to offend him?*

Nothing came to mind, but there must have been something. His manner had been more than plain. Even now, she could see him playing a game of croquet with Miss Bainbridge, a pained expression on his face. It was clear that he did not want to be there, playing that game.

And yet, he is doing it. Oh, if I were a duke – even if I were a man – I'd never suffer my way through any nonsense like this. I should do what I liked. I should say what I liked.

Lavinia was so lost in her sour thoughts that she didn't hear the other woman approaching until she flopped down beside her on the blanket.

"Penny for them," Katherine said, grinning.

"I... I beg your pardon?"

"Penny for your thoughts," Katherine repeated. "You looked entirely lost in thought. They must be interesting, then. Your thoughts."

Lavinia grimaced. "Quite the contrary, I'm afraid. They're rather uncharitable. I'd rather forget them myself."

Katherine nodded, making herself more comfortable. "I saw you sitting here alone, and thought that we could have a little talk, you and I."

"What an ominous way to start a conversation."

Katherine gave a sharp laugh. "Oh, you are quite the wit, Miss Brookford. I mean that in the most flattering manner, as you surely comprehend. You express your thoughts with such candour."

"More often than I should."

She shrugged. "It's a refreshing sort of honesty. One doesn't see it a great deal in Society."

"I... I believe your brother said something similar to me, once."

She nodded thoughtfully. "Yes. William, on occasions, is either the cleverest man I have ever met, or the most foolish. It is as if he cannot make up his mind."

Lavinia had to bite back a smile at that. "You are his sister; it is your prerogative to be ungenerous."

"Spoken like a sibling yourself. You have only a sister, is that right, Miss Brookford? No brothers?"

Lavinia's face fell. The familiar nausea and misery lodged itself in her gut. She looked away.

"Only Gillian," she responded, voice quiet. When she looked back, Katherine was watching her, a furrow between her brows.

"Forgive me," she said at last. "I... I believe I have overstepped. I've upset you."

Lavinia shook her head. "It's nothing, truly. It's no secret, I think, that I do not feel particularly comfortable in this sort of Society. House gatherings are not my forte. But you have been so kind to me. I don't think I would be doing either of us a service if I were to take offence now."

Katherine watched her carefully, pursing her lips. "You are very generous."

"I am never quite as generous as I should be."

"I suppose none of us are. But that is not why I came over here, Miss Brookford."

Lavinia lifted an eyebrow. "Pray, continue. Share with me the nature of your enigmatic undertaking."

Katherine grinned. "Straight to the point. I like it. The thing is, Miss Brookford, I want to talk to you about William."

She flinched, despite herself. "T-The duke?"

"He isn't the duke to me, my dear. The thing about William, is that he's... well, he's something of a mystery. He gets the oddest ideas in his head, and once they'd lodged in there, there isn't much a person can do about it."

"I noticed as much," Lavinia mumbled, before she could stop herself. She glanced up and found Katherine looking at her again, a sort of knowing look on her face.

She saw him snub me, Lavinia thought, heart sinking. It was a little embarrassing, but she was getting good at swallowing embarrassments these days.

"Don't give up on him, Lavinia," Katherine said abruptly. "You... you seem to be good for him. I know my brother, and I know how he can't stand the falseness and silliness of the Season. He wants an anchor, somebody he can rely upon. Somebody who sees him for who he is, not the Duke of Dunleigh. I feel that some other ladies — although they might be better suited to the role of duchess — may not *see* him correctly, if you know what I mean. They may not understand him. I am not looking for a duchess for my brother, Miss Brookford. I am looking for his wife. A life partner. Somebody who will make him happy, and somebody that *he* can make happy. I have seen what it is like, for a married couple that are not well-suited. It is upsetting. It is unfortunate. It generally cannot be remedied. I don't want that for William."

Katherine let out a long breath at the end of this speech, leaning back to gauge its effect on Lavinia.

She took her time before responding, a little shocked at the forthrightness of this speech. And at a picnic, no less, with all of their friends and guests around!

"It can't have been easy for you to say all of that," she managed at last. It felt like a rather feeble thing to say, but it was better than nothing, after all.

Katherine only grinned. "Oh, yes, it's a most shocking speech. I rehearsed some of it in my head before I came over here. You aren't offended, I hope, by any of it?"

Lavinia shook her head. "No, of course not. But I think... I think perhaps you have misinterpreted the relationship between the duke and myself. He is a fine man, but I am sure he sees me as nothing but a good acquaintance."

Katherine looked away, a smile playing over her lips.

"Perhaps. Perhaps not. As I said, Miss Brookford, please don't give up on him. He's a fool, sometimes, but things have happened to him to make him that way. He's a fine man with a prickly exterior."

"Like a hedgehog."

Lavinia wasn't entirely sure where that comment had come from. She rather wished she hadn't said it, but of course it was too late now. Katherine suppressed a smile.

"Yes, Miss Brookford. Exactly like a hedgehog. You take my meaning, though, I think?"

She bit her lip, glancing down. "Yes. Yes, I think I do. I only hope you aren't placing too much faith in me. You overestimate me."

Katherine climbed to her feet, shaking stray pieces of grass from her skirt.

"Miss Brookford, you underestimate yourself. Good day."

With that, she walked off, leaving Lavinia with her head spinning.

Chapter Seventeen

"You've behaved badly, Will. Very badly, indeed!"

Katherine's words rang in his head. William stood in front of his dressing-room mirror, angrily tying his cravat. What had possessed him to dismiss his valet so soon? He *had* been dressed, but endless fidgeting with his cravat had made the linen lose its sharpness and droop, obliging him to untie it and choose a fresh one. And now his fingers would not work, and the knot simply would *not* sit.

He should have known that Katherine would have something to say about the situation. He *hadn't* snubbed Miss Brookford, not really. He'd simply... simply avoided her.

Wasn't that sensible? His own feelings had taken him by surprise. If anything, their meeting at the horse paddock had shown him that he was becoming distracted from the woman he *should* be pursuing – Miss Bainbridge – and that simply wouldn't do.

Miss Bainbridge is the choice I have made. She's perfect for the Duchess of Dunleigh. Why would I choose anyone else? And it's certainly not fair to give Miss Brookford false hope. Well, not false, *exactly, as my feelings towards her are.... Again, this matters not at all. I cannot marry her. She's not suitable for a duchess. Even... even if I felt differently, I am tied to Miss Bainbridge now. The thing is done. Soon an announcement will follow, and then that will be that. It isn't Miss Brookford's fault. It is mine.*

His hands dropped from the knotted mess of his cravat. His hair was wild – he must have run his fingers through it at some point – and the overall effect was entirely too *dishabille* for a dinner party. His mother would be thoroughly displeased if she found him in the dining room presented in such a manner.

Sighing, he moved over to the bell pull at the corner of the room. It was a pity to summon the poor man back after he'd been dismissed, but really...

A gentle knock sounded on the door. William paused, hand inches from the bell pull.

"Who is it?"

"It is I, William. May I come in?"

He crossed the room at once, pulling open the door.

"Mother? What are you doing here?"

Mary was dressed for dinner. She wore a long lawn gown in dark blue, decorated with pearls and a few diamonds. The candlelight made her look younger and less gaunt than before.

William stood there for a moment, staring. Had his mother ever visited his room before? He couldn't recall if she had. He certainly never visited *hers*, not even as a child. He wasn't even sure he could find his way to her room.

"Mother," he managed again. "What is it?"

Mary blinked, waking herself up from a reverie. "Oh, I came to talk to you. Might I come in?"

"I... Of course. I am about to ring for my valet, though. My cravat is undone."

Mary glanced at the wrinkled mess of linen at her son's throat and sighed.

"I shall tie it for you."

William blinked. "What?"

Mary slipped past him, stepping into the room. William closed the door after her, feeling as awkward as a child. He placed his hands behind his back, decided that it was a silly position, and after a moment, let them hang by his sides.

His mother went straight to the wardrobe, selecting a fresh-pressed piece of linen.

"Katherine spoke to me," she said, after a pause. "I ought to be closer to my only daughter, I know that. Alexander's wife – Abigail – says as much. I hold Abigail in high regard. She possesses a commendable sense and is remarkably considerate."

William pressed his lips together. "Did you come here to tell me how much you prefer your daughter-in-law to your true daughter, Mother?"

That was entirely too sharp, and he could have bitten off his tongue as soon as the words were out. Mary, however, did not seem upset. She only came over to him, deftly untying the knot of his cravat and tossing the ruined linen again.

"My point," she said, carefully sliding the fresh piece of linen around his neck, "is that Katherine rarely asks me for favours. Never, in fact. So, in light of Abigail's rather stern advice, I have listened to Katherine carefully. I am here to speak to you about the matter of your marriage, William."

He deflated. Of course, his mother had not simply come to see him. She had come to lecture him some more. Part of him longed to tell her that she had no need to worry about that, as he was engaged to Miss Bainbridge, and that was that. He couldn't tell her, of course, as the secret engagement would quickly become public.

"I am not in the mood, Mother. Pray, from whence did you acquire the skill to don a cravat?" He observed, seeking to shift the discourse.

"My brother could never quite master it, and in our youth, we were rather impoverished. Our circumstances shifted, indeed, and quite dramatically, but for a time, we had to learn to attire ourselves and arrange our own coiffures. My brother would assist me in securing my tresses, and I would knot his cravat. It functioned admirably."

William had never heard this before. He blinked down at his mother, wondering if he knew the woman at all.

"I... I had no idea, Mother."

"Well, once we were married, your father never wanted me to talk about my old life. About the hardships we encountered. You see, your father married me because he thought I would make a good duchess. I was well-bred, of one of the oldest families in England. I was graceful, shy, thoughtful, beautiful. I did make a good duchess, so I suppose he chose wisely there. But I married him for love, and I thought things would work out in the end. Sometimes such marriages work. Mine, I suppose, did not."

She let out a long, slow sigh. Her fingers worked deftly, manoeuvring the stiff linen into a simple, plain cravat knot, more than suitable for a dinner party with dancing afterwards.

"I never really stopped loving your father," Mary continued, a slight frown appearing between her brows. "It would have been easier, I think, if I had, but one has so little control over these things. Marriage is a most intricate affair, William, even when one selects the most suitable partner. I daresay you may surmise the nature of my counsel."

"Are you about to tell me to follow my heart, Mother?" William managed. His mouth had gone dry, and he had to put some effort in order to speak.

Mary made a little *sound*. "I am about to tell you to choose *wisely*. You aim to marry the Bainbridge girl? Very good, she's a wise choice. She will make a fine duchess. But there must be more, William. Any woman can make a *suitable* wife, but more is required. More is always required. Do you have any intentions of pursuing Miss Lavinia?"

"Mother!"

"She is not at all suited for the role of duchess," Mary continued, as if he had not spoken, "but she might learn, if your wish was to engage into matrimony with her." If she had the same strong feelings for you that you had for her. There are many contingencies and considerations to a matrimonial union, William. You cannot simply pick a woman based on one or two qualities, or because you think you *ought* to pick her. I cannot make that decision for you. Neither can Katherine, or your brothers, or the Bainbridges. Only you can choose. And decisions you make, even in haste, will affect the rest of your life. But *only if you let them.* Do you understand?"

She stepped back, letting her hands drop. Feeling rather as if he were in a dream, William turned to look at himself in the mirror.

His cravat was knotted neatly, every bit as efficiently and cleverly as his valet had managed. He wanted to lift a hand to worry the linen between his fingertips but forced himself to keep his hands down.

"Thank you, Mother," William managed at last. "For… for the advice, and for the cravat."

She nodded. "I am not a *complete* failure of a mother, you see."

He turned, smiling nervously. "You… your dress is very pretty, Mother. It rather reminds me of Lady Brennon's gown."

Mary smoothed it out with her hands, going pink. "Yes, I thought her gown looked pretty on her and I considered trying something like that for myself."

"For what it's worth — of course I have no say over your friends, Mother — I very much approve of this friendship with Lady Brennon. She is an excellent friend for you."

Mary smiled shyly, almost like a woman decades younger.

"I do like her very much. It is pleasant to have a real friend again."

"I wish you luck, Mother. Not that you need it, of course."

She nodded and turned to go. Their conversation, it seemed, was over. William was sure that once his mother had left the room, they would go back to their usual, distant relationship, more like polite acquaintances than mother and son. But they would always have this, wouldn't they? A neatly tied cravat and some well-worded advice.

Mary paused, one hand on the doorknob.

"Oh, there was something else, I nearly forgot. Katherine said that you're to apologise to Miss Brookford. She said that you would know what that meant. What *does* it mean, William? I hope you haven't insulted the girl."

He bit back a smile. "Not exactly, but I do owe her an apology. Katherine is very astute. Would you kindly convey to Katherine, on my behalf, that if she does not cease her unwelcome interference in my affairs, I shall be compelled to take decisive action?"

Mary pursed her lips, face heavy with disapproval.

"No, William, I shall not tell her that. Do dress quickly and come on downstairs. And you must dance tonight – it will be expected of you."

He nodded, ducking his head. "I will, Mother. And… and thank you. For everything."

Mary gave a tiny nod and a tinier smile. Ducking out into the hallway and closing the door behind her, she disappeared.

William turned back to his own reflection, inspecting the cravat. For the first time, he wondered whether their family might be contacted again. While the old duke was alive, it was out of the question, but now...

A subject for later, he told himself firmly, smoothing down his hair. *For now, concentrate on securing a duchess and your fortune, and then we can think about our extended family. It's likely that they wouldn't want anything to do with us, and I'm not sure I can blame them.*

And then the supper-gong rang, and William cursed to himself and hurried out to join his guests.

***

There was to be music and dancing after dinner, and so the ballroom was filled with a flurry of activity. Servants were doing last-minute cleaning and dusting, polishing up the floors to a high shine, setting garlands and vases of flowers here and there.

William moved through the ballroom to check that all was in order, on his way to the dining room. Already, Miss Bainbridge had dropped hints about dancing with him. He would have to ask her. There was no sense in offending the Bainbridges, and one dance couldn't hurt, surely?

Famous last words, he thought, hiding a smile. Miss Bainbridge was growing desperate. The fault was entirely his. He ought to be plain with her and decisive with himself. He should *decide*, and allow Miss Bainbridge or Miss Brookford to seek other husbands, and forget all about him.

I don't deserve either of them, he thought miserably.

The preparations were all well in hand, and so he was obliged to exit the ballroom and head towards the dining room, where the rest of the guests were gathering. He could hear the laughter and chatter from all the way down the hall.

Sighing, he put down his head and broke into a light jog. It wouldn't do for him to be late, after all.

Then a woman in a pale lavender gown stepped out in front of him, head turned away. She was still fixing pins into her hair, a handful of pearl-topped decorative pins sticking out of her mouth. He narrowly avoided bumping into her.

It was, of course, Miss Brookford.

She turned around, an apology – and the pins – lingering on her lips, and the colour drained from her face when she saw him.

"Oh, your Grace," she managed at last. "I do apologise. I didn't see you there."

"The fault is mine."

She gave a brief nod, rapidly shoving the last of the pins into her hair and turned to leave.

"Stay a moment," he blurted out, before he could stop himself.

She glanced back at him, expression guarded. "Is something amiss, your Grace?"

He drew in a breath. "Yes, there is something wrong. I... I was unaccountably rude to you at the picnic. I snubbed you, and you were nothing but friendly to me. I apologise."

She bit her lip, searching his face for something. "It is quite acceptable. I harbour no ill feelings. I am not angry. You should not feel obliged..."

"I don't feel obliged to do anything. I am sorry, Miss Brookford. I don't know what possessed me. I... In fact, I planned to ask you whether you would dance with me tonight."

She blinked, clearly taken aback. "Oh. I did not expect... that is to say... I would be honoured to dance with you."

He smiled, a little shaken by the strength of his relief. "I'm glad. Which sets do you have free?"

She inspected her dance card and let out a huff of laughter. "At the moment? All of them."

Chapter Eighteen

Miss Bainbridge was positively seething, that much was for sure. The duke had danced with her, alright, but only a sedate, matronly sort of jig. It was a slow, dull dance, full of partners who were dancing together out of duty or obligation.

The duke had asked Lavinia to dance the waltz with him.

She hadn't realized it at the time, not until the music started up and he came to claim her.

It was odd, dancing the waltz. This would be the second time she'd danced the waltz with the Duke of Dunleigh, and that would be noticed. Eyes were all set on Lavinia as she swirled around the room with him, the skirts of her gown swinging out and glittering.

Miss Bainbridge had chosen a deep red velvet gown, cut in the latest style. It was a pretty enough dress, and suited her, but the colour – which she had doubtless intended to be striking and mature among a seat of pastel-coloured gowns – simply made her seem dark and dull. She did not stand out, and a handful of serious old matrons had chosen the same shade of dark red. Velvet was also a popular material amongst the widows.

Lavinia bit back a giggle at this thought. She didn't mean Miss Bainbridge any harm. Under different circumstances, they might even have been friends. But it was pretty clear that Miss Bainbridge wanted the duke – or, more to the point, she wanted to be a duchess – and since she considered Lavinia as a rival, they could not possibly be friends. She'd taken every opportunity to make Lavinia feel silly and small, and so it was hard not to feel a little triumph.

"You seem distracted," the duke remarked, when Lavinia nearly trod on his foot.

Serves me right, she thought wryly, *for being too triumphant over Miss Bainbridge. He's probably still going to marry* her, *at the end of the day.*

"I'm tired," she said, and it wasn't exactly a lie.

"I'm sorry. I shouldn't have made you dance."

"No, no, I didn't mean that. I..." she paused, biting her lip, and forced herself to meet his eye. "I'm enjoying myself. Truly, I am. I'm glad we're friends again."

Was that too much? Was she presuming that they had ever *been* friends *to begin with?* Any doubts Lavinia had were wiped away when the duke smiled, slowly and almost shyly.

"I'm glad," he said, voice quiet. "I'm glad we're friends again, too."

She beamed.

***

Lavinia woke up to a strip of sunlight shining directly onto her eyes. She'd been wrapped up in a lovely dream about the dinner party last night.

It was *a triumph. Me, dancing the waltz with the duke again, Gillian and her Lord Langley staring dotingly at each other all night. Miss Bainbridge's palpable rage. Yes, it was a success.*

She squinted at the sunlight, streaming through a crack in the curtains. Her feet were still sore from all the dancing she'd done last night. Once it was clear that the duke wanted to dance with her, suddenly all the other gentlemen wanted to stand up with her, too. She'd danced with Lord Langley too, of course, but that was just to please Gillian. He was a pleasant enough man, and Lavinia thought she would like to see him as her brother-in-law.

She sat up, stifling a yawn. The house, as far as she could tell, was silent. A glance at the sky outside revealed that it was probably no later than seven o' clock in the morning. The servants would be up and about, of course, but most of the guests would still be resting after their late night. Perhaps a couple of early risers would be taking breakfast – the Bainbridges, she'd be willing to bet – but most of them would not appear until close to noon.

Lavinia debated lying back down again. A few more hours of sleep would do her good.

Somehow, though, she had plenty of energy, and sleep did not seem quite so appealing. She lowered herself back onto her elbows, peering up at the canopy.

It didn't take her long to decide.

Flinging back the covers, Lavinia hopped out of bed. She washed and dressed quickly, not bothering to ring for a maid. Last night's dress was spread out in front of the wardrobe, ready to be washed, pressed, and replaced. Her dancing slippers were set side by side beside it, the toes scuffed and the soles more worn than any dancing slippers she'd worn before.

Grinning to herself, Lavinia pulled out a worn old dress, plain brown, easy to get on by herself. She took out a pair of riding boots to go with it, and carelessly pinned up her hair on top of her head, not caring about the few locks that fell down around her ears. It wasn't as if anybody was going to see her.

Yes, an early morning ride was just the ticket. She missed Stepper. Her mother, of course, would disapprove. So would Gillian, as a matter of fact. Sneaking out to go riding alone was bad enough when one was at home, but when one was a guest at a house party like this one, it was much worse.

Nobody will know, she reminded herself. *It doesn't matter.*

Already thrilling with excitement at her own little adventure, Lavinia slipped out into the hallway. She would put her boots on at the door. No sense in being overheard and caught out before her adventure had even started.

***

Stepper was clearly thrilled to go for a ride. He fidgeted as Lavinia saddled him up, tossing his head and rubbing his nose against her shoulder. She shushed him, keeping her eyes peeled for a groom. They might insist on coming with her, or else send word to that disapproving butler.

Or worse, her mother.

Lavinia led Stepper out of the stable, saddled and bridled and ready to go. She was already planning out her route in her head. They would ride up the hills, to where the mist still clung to the damp ground, and the sky was so heavy and grey it seemed to be about to touch the summits. The view from up there had to be spectacular.

She stopped dead at the sight of a man, sitting on a bench with his back to her, facing the horse paddocks. She could see that, in one of the distant paddocks, the beautiful black stallion was cropping grass.

She froze. *Can I sneak past him?*

On cue, Stepper snorted loudly, and pawed the ground, annoyed at the delay. The man tensed and twisted around to look behind him.

It should not have come as a surprise for her to see that it was the duke. He, at least, seemed equally surprised to see her. He jumped to his feet and made a neat bow.

"Miss Brookford. I apologise, I didn't... didn't know that anyone was here."

She bit her lip. He must have arrived minutes after her, since the courtyard had been empty when she arrived.

"It's alright. I hope I'm not disturbing your..." she trailed off, not entirely sure what it was he was doing. "I was just going out for a ride."

"Oh. I see." He eyed Stepper nervously. Annoyed with the delay, the horse tossed his head, tugging on the reins in Lavinia's hand.

On impulse, she led him over to the fence, wrapping the reins around a post. Stepper gave a snort of annoyance, then resigned himself to cropping the grass at the bottom of the fence post.

She edged towards the duke, who was still standing awkwardly beside the bench.

"Why don't you come with me?"

He flinched, eyes wide. "What, on your horse?"

"Well, no. You'd need your own horse."

He glanced over at the stallion.

"Not that one," she added hastily. "A nice, tame mare from the stables. I've seen some of them bear children on their backs. You'd be safe."

"It's... it's not that I'm a coward, I just..."

"I don't think you're a coward," Lavinia said firmly. "Fear is entirely natural, and whoever says otherwise is just a simpleton. "My brother, Hugh, was afraid of horses, and he was a remarkably brave man."

There was a brief moment of silence between them. Hugh's name seemed to hang in the air. It prickled over

Lavinia's skin. When was the last time she'd spoken his name aloud? Oh, he was always on her mind, his name and face always going round and round in her head. But she felt that if she spoke his name aloud, it would start up the pain again. The pain of grief and loss, she'd learned, never quite went away.

The duke looked away. "I didn't mean to offend you."

"You... you didn't."

"Your brother... he is not... not with you? I had heard that you had only one sister. But... my sister told me that there was a tragedy about your brother."

She looked him full in the face and gave a bleak smile. "There is just the two of us, now."

The duke understood and dropped his gaze. "I am sorry. I have never lost a sibling, and I can't... cannot imagine how it would feel."

"It feels... as though the bottom has dropped out of one's world," Lavinia said, voice so quiet she could barely even hear it herself. "Hugh was a remarkable man. He was kind, fair, handsome, charming, and so intelligent. I said once that my parents — my mother, at least — favour Gillian over me. It was never like that when Hugh was alive. He brought balance to our family, it seemed. He used to love giving presents, I remember that much," she paused, chuckling at the memories which came flooding in. "He would bring back trinkets for us whenever he went away, silly tin necklaces and wooden rings and carved animals, things like that. He'd wrap them up so carefully, and hide them in our beds, so that we would find them when we went to bed. I remember once he bought me some books he knew I wanted and slipped them under my pillow. I was tired, and threw myself into bed without checking, and banged my head on a pile of books. I was fairly cursing him; I can tell you."

The duke chuckled. "He sounds like a kind man."

"He was, he was. He loved getting presents, too. He would get as excited as a child. I often wish now that I'd given him more things. I never thought about it, at the time."

"How old was your brother, when you... when you lost him?" the duke seemed to have difficulty getting out the words. Lavinia wondered which of his siblings he was imagining losing.

"Twenty," she said at last. "Just turned twenty. He was the oldest of the three of us. He was never strong. When he was young, a horse threw him and broke his arm. It could have happened to anyone, and his arm healed well, but he refused to ride again or have anything to do with horses. Papa loves horses, and is interested in breeding horses, and he'd always intended for Hugh to help him with that. I think the day Hugh told him he intended to go into the law was the only time I've heard the two of them argue."

She sighed, looking down. "Papa always thought he'd change his mind, but once Hugh started learning the law, that would be the end of that. They parted on bad terms. Hugh went to London and began his studies. He excelled, from what I heard. But as I said, he was not strong, and London is... well, you know what it's like. And of course, Hugh was not staying in the good part of London. He'd taken on cheap lodgings. You must already know that we are not a rich family anymore, and those lodgings were all Hugh could afford. He had been studying for about six months when he got ill. He stayed quiet about his illness for a while, thinking that it would clear up. When it became clear that he was seriously ill, and could no longer afford the physician's fees, he travelled home to us."

Lavinia paused, wiping away a tear with the back of her hand. She was a little shaken at how powerfully the story had affected her. The duke said nothing, eyes fixed on her face, waiting for her to continue.

"He died a week after coming home," she finished at last, voice shaking. "We tried to nurse him, paid for all the best physicians, but it was too late. The sickness had taken his lungs, you see. When he arrived home, he looked like a ghost. I don't think I'll ever forget his pale, gaunt face. And just like that," she snapped her fingers, "the light of our lives was extinguished. I used to have a locket," she paused, tapping her collarbone where Hugh's locket would lie, "with a picture of Hugh as a child in it. I lost it at a ball one night. I remember always taking it for granted, and then one day it was gone forever. My last piece of Hugh. Gone. The clasp broke, I imagine."

The duke flinched at that. Perhaps the image of a lost locket was too powerful for him to resist. She drew in a breath and continued.

"My point is, your Grace, life waits for nobody. Things can change in an instant. Allowing fear to rule us can be fatal – we have no idea what waits around the corner. Your father is gone. Dead. So is Hugh. We, however, are not."

He swallowed hard. "And what is your purpose in saying all that, Miss Brookford?"

She smiled wryly, swallowing back the familiar tide of grief. "I am saying that you should ride a horse again, your Grace. Today. Now. After all, tomorrow we may all be dead."

He sighed. "What a cheerful notion."

"I am just being honest."

He breathed in deeply, squaring his shoulders. She saw him glance across the paddocks to the glistening black stallion.

"Very well," he said at last. "I will go riding with you."

Chapter Nineteen

For one awful, heart-stopping moment, William thought that she was going to suggest that he ride the stallion.

He wasn't entirely sure what he would have done if she did. Faint, perhaps? Was he going to swoon, right there on the stable courtyard?

The panic only lasted a second. Lavinia headed back towards the stable, jerking her head for him to follow.

"We can't go alone," William said, finding himself following. "I'll ask a groom to accompany us."

"If you like."

He flagged down a passing stable boy, the lad's eyes betraying his surprise when he saw William and Miss Brookford.

"This one should suit you," Miss Brookford said, leading out a sedate-looking chestnut mare. He vaguely recognized the horse as an old favourite of Katherine's.

"I... I am not sure I can do this, after all," William stammered, eyeing the mare's high back.

"Well, I shan't insist, to be sure," Miss Brookford said briskly, fetching a saddle down from its hook. "But let's just saddle up the mare and go outside, and see how you feel, then. What do you say?"

He bit back a sigh. "Very well, very well."

It was easiest to step back and simply let her get on with saddling up the mare, who stood mildly by. Miss Brookford's horse – Stepper, wasn't it? – watched in interest.

At last the mare – somewhere in his memory he recalled that her name was Cinnamon – was saddled up and ready, and waited patiently for her rider.

"Well, there it is," Miss Brookford said. Lavinia. Her name was Lavinia. For some reason, it seemed more important to think of her as *Lavinia* than as Miss Brookford. "Why don't you try and sit on her back, at least?"

He drew in a breath. She'd told him that she wouldn't insist, and he was fairly sure that she would not. If he decided to return to the house now, she would not say a word.

Life is short. What will I have achieved if I turn back now?

Suddenly, William knew that if he did not climb on the horse now, today, he would never climb one again.

Drawing in a breath, he took a step towards the mare. She did not rear or roll her eyes, only watched his progress with mild interest. Miss Brookford slid a small mounting block towards the horse with her foot. He glared at her.

"I can get up without a mounting block, Miss Brookford."

"I'm sure you can," she answered, cheerfully. "But it will make things easier, don't you think? Why don't you give the mare some treats?"

"I haven't anything."

"Don't worry. I thought ahead."

She dug into a pocket and withdrew some browning apple slices, handing them over to William. The mare's ears flicked in interest. He extended his hand, a piece of apple resting on his palm. The mare leaned delicately forward, lipping at his skin, and seemed to *inhale* the piece of apple. She crunched happily, and William held his breath and touched the soft, warm hair along her nose.

"Hello, there, girl," he managed at last, in the sort of soothing tone he thought that horses were meant to enjoy. "You're a pretty one, eh?"

He was vaguely conscious of activity behind him, a groom preparing a horse to follow them, but the mare didn't seem distracted at all. She watched him with large, liquid eyes, patiently waiting for what came next.

"You can do it, your Grace," Miss Brookford said softly. "If anyone can do it, you can."

Your Grace. What a clunky title. It wasn't really a name at all. He'd heard her use his name before, and how wonderful it had sounded, coming from her.

Stop it, he thought angrily, pushing away the thoughts. *This is about you getting on that wretched horse.*

He immediately felt guilty for thinking of the poor mare in such angry terms. It wasn't *her* fault.

Drawing in a deep breath, he placed one hand on the warm leather of the saddle, put his opposite foot in the stirrup, and hauled himself up, just like he'd done a few times in the past before his father died.

The mare barely shifted under his weight. He wondered briefly if she knew that he was on her at all. Heart pounding with dread, William clutched at the reins, hastily fitting his other foot into the other stirrup.

And then it was done. He was on the horse. Cinnamon twisted around to look at him, then ducked her head to crop at a patch of grass.

"Nicely done," Miss Brookford said. She did sound genuinely impressed. "You seem to be a good rider."

"How can you tell that from my sitting in the saddle?"

"Ah, a good seat on a horse is the key to it all."

She climbed nimbly up onto her own horse, who pranced with delight at the prospect of finally setting off.

"Shall we?" she asked, lifting her eyebrows at William.

He paused, glancing down at the horse's neck. The creature seemed entirely content to stand still. She made no sudden movements, no signs of irritation that he was on her back, and certainly no bucking or jerking.

Tentatively, William tapped his heels against the horse's sides. She moved forward at once at a slow, rolling walk. Despite himself, he gave a squawk and clutched at the reins.

Miss Brookford chuckled, falling into step beside him.

"And how do you feel?"

"Well, I don't feel excellent. I feel a little sick, to be frank, but it's... it's not as bad as I thought it was going to be."

"I'm glad."

They followed the fence which encircled the courtyard, all the way to where the gate gaped open, and a gravel path led up towards steep hills. He glanced over at Miss Brookford, whose profile was turned towards him and her gaze fixed on the road ahead, and a wave of powerful affection washed over him.

I love you.

No, I mustn't. I mustn't.

Perhaps sensing his gaze on her, she glanced over and gave him a smile.

"Do you feel up to something a little faster?"

"I... I don't know..." he stammered.

Behind them, the groom gave a squawk. He had barely begun saddling up the horse, and seemed a trifle horrified to see Miss Brookford and his master moving away.

"Wait a moment, your Grace, wait a moment!"

Miss Brookford met his eye and grinned mischievously.

"Shall we?"

There was no time to ask what she meant. Miss Brookford tapped her horse's flanks with the heels, and immediately the creature broke into a run, head straining joyfully forward.

William could have stopped Cinnamon from following. He remembered enough about how to check a horse, how to handle the reins, and how to sit.

He didn't.

Cinnamon lurched forward, following her new friend, and William sucked in a deep, surprised breath.

How long had it been since he'd ridden a horse? He hadn't always hated it. Fear sparked sharply in his gut, and he leaned forward automatically, clutching the reins. The horse sped up, faster and faster until he knew without a doubt that it was the mare who was in control, not him.

Miss Brookford and Stepper raced ahead, her skirts and hair billowing out behind her.

Abruptly, the path levelled out, and William realized with a pang of surprise that they were there, they had reached the summit.

And, of course, that they were alone. The shouting groom was long gone, left behind. William couldn't see any signs that they were being followed.

Miss Brookford slowed her horse to a brisk trot, and Cinnamon slowed accordingly. William let out a breath he didn't even know he had been holding, his lungs burning. Sweat beaded on his forehead, sticking his hair down to his scalp. Lifting a shaking hand to his face, he wiped away sweat.

They slowed even more, finally stopping when the summit flattened out into a plateau.

"Well," Miss Brookford said, sounding breathless, "You did it. Here we are."

Letting out a shaky breath, he risked a look around. The view was spectacular, his own grounds spreading out below, the eaves of the houses far, far below. He wasn't sure whether he wanted to laugh or cry. He wanted to say something, but his words seemed to have deserted him.

In the end, the decision was made for him. The overcast clouds seemed to give a shudder, suddenly darkening with rain. Miss Brookford glanced up and winced.

"Oh, dear. I think perhaps we'd better head down again, before we get caught in the rain."

A lock of her hair had come loose, hanging around her face. William couldn't help but stare at it.

"Yes," he managed at last. "Perhaps we should."

Chapter Twenty

The first few fat drops of rain started to fall as they neared the bottom of the hill.

Lavinia had kept a close eye on the duke, making sure that he was safe and well. It had occurred to her, more than once, that perhaps she'd been a little too hasty, strong-arming him into riding a horse before he was ready.

Her doubts had been put to rest fairly quickly. It was clear that the duke, despite his fears and misgivings, was in fact a good rider. Muscle memory for a thing like that tended to remain. The mare was a steady, good horse, and William sat well in his saddle. Their descent was much slower than their ascent, with William gripping the reins a little tighter than before, his face pale. Lavinia kept pace with him, talking easily and lightly about everything and nothing, mostly to distract him from his own fears, which were doubtless clamouring for attention.

He managed well, straight-backed and clearly nervous, but keeping his composure and keeping control of the reins.

For a first ride, she thought wryly, *we certainly started out in a hurry. Perhaps I should have only let him sit on the horse, and get used to that, before we galloped up a hill.*

She wanted to laugh. It had worked, though, hadn't it?

Back in the courtyard, the groom waited, arms folded and his lips pressed tight in disapproval.

"I thought you wanted me to accompany you, your Grace," he said, as soon as they were within earshot, clearly annoyed. "You didn't wait. I was concerned about you, your Grace. Anything could have happened."

William had the grace to look embarrassed. "I am sorry, John. We ought to have waited. Next time, I will, I promise."

"The fault was mine," Lavinia confessed, leaping nimbly down. "I hurried his Grace away. I apologise, as well."

The groom looked a little mollified. "As you say, your Grace, your ladyship."

A gong rang out distantly in the house. Wincing, Lavinia turned to William.

"I had better go in. My mother might have noticed my absence. She'll worry, I think."

He nodded, something odd in his face that she could not quite identify. She had caught him looking at her several times during their ride and convinced herself that it was only to see what she was doing, so that he might copy her.

Now, it seemed... well, she thought it might be something else. Warmth spread through her chest.

The moment was ruined by the groom coughing pointedly.

"Shall I take the horses in, your Grace?"

William blinked, seeming to recover himself. "Yes, yes, of course. Thank you, John."

Smiling nervously, Lavinia handed over Stepper's reins and turned towards the house. A movement at an upper window caught her attention, but aside from the flick of a dove-grey skirt, she could not see who had been looking down at her, or even if they had seen her or not. Perhaps it was just a servant passing by.

Lavinia bit her lip, an uneasy feeling starting up in her gut. She put her head down and began to walk faster. If she hurried, she might get inside before the rain started in earnest.

She was not quite correct.

A mere ten feet from the steps, the heavens truly opened, forcing Lavinia to sprint the remaining distance, her shawl held over her head. She stumbled inside, panting for breath, flushed with the exercise and her own adventure, wanting to laugh aloud.

"Lavinia!"

She flinched at her mother's voice.

"Oh, Mama. I did not see you there."

Lady Brennon stood in the hallway, wearing a neat little morning-dress of blue velvet. It clashed with her face, which was crimson.

"Where have you *been*?" she hissed. "Imagine my consternation when I discovered you were gone from your bed! Were you riding? You were, weren't you? Oh, you wretched girl. You are so thoughtless!"

"I'm sorry, Mama. Have I missed breakfast?"

"Yes, and the Dowager has decided that all of us ladies will gather in the morning-room and spend a quiet morning together, on account of the rain. Your absence is conspicuous, let me tell you. Go on in at once."

"I need to change!" Lavinia glanced down at her damp dress. It wasn't *too* crumpled, and she couldn't see any noticeable stains. Her hair, however, was another story.

Lady Brennon gave a huff of annoyance and started shouting at her daughter.

"You can't," she said shortly. "There's no time."

Using her fingers, she was able to comb Lavinia's hair into some semblance of a style, repining the loose locks and twisting it back into something neater.

"That will have to do," she murmured, casting a disapproving look over Lavinia's rumpled gown. "You smell of horse, but not overwhelmingly so. The flush in your cheeks is quite scandalous, but I'm sure it will subside soon enough.

Don't let anyone near enough to smell you. Go on, in you go, in you go!"

Lavinia was hustled along the corridors and abruptly shoved into a large, airy room, full of women. Some ladies sat reading by the window, others sewed on the long sofa, and still more clustered around the fireplace and by the refreshments tables, chatting in low, sedate voices. A good number of them looked up as Lady Brennon and Lavinia walked in.

"Goodness," came a familiar voice which Lavinia was starting to heartily dislike, "what a sluggard you are, Miss Brookford! We'd quite given you up for lost."

She forced a smile. "Good morning, Miss Bainbridge. I must confess myself quite tired this morning. I am sorry not to join you all sooner."

Miss Bainbridge came rustling forward, and Lavinia's smile dropped as she noticed her gown. Her dove-grey gown.

She met Miss Bainbridge's eye and saw something flicker there that she did not like.

The moment crackled, seeming to go on forever, before Lady Brennon yanked Lavinia unceremoniously away, dragging her over to a quiet, low stool in the corner of the room.

"Sit here and try not to speak to anyone," Lady Brennon hissed. "You can change before luncheon, before we go out to the Assembly Rooms, but it'll look odd if you change before. Sit here for half an hour and then excuse yourself."

Lavinia bit her lip and said nothing. It seemed that no response was needed, really. Her mother rustled away, joining the dowager duchess on a two-seater sofa. The soft undertone of voices started up again, and Lavinia shifted, getting ready to sink into boredom for a while. Something caught her eye, and she surreptitiously bent over to peer at her dress.

Her heart sank. There was a large, fist-shaped splash of mud on her skirt, just above her hem. It stood out on the plain fabric, and Lavinia hastily arranged the material in a way that ought to hide it. The stain was too large, however, and any reckless movement would display the stain.

Questions would naturally follow. Where had she gone? A walk? A ride? Who with? *Alone*? Oh, shocking, shocking!

The truth would be worse. Not alone, but with the duke? That would destroy Lavinia's reputation forever.

Half an hour, she told herself, glancing at the clock. *I can manage half an hour, surely.*

On cue, a particular young woman detached herself from the group and headed towards Lavinia, smiling in a rather malicious way.

"Why, Miss Brookford, here you are sitting out of the way! How dull for you!" Miss Bainbridge cooed, revealing white, sharp teeth. "I shall sit by you."

There was really nothing for Lavinia to say to that. She smiled tightly, cursing her luck, as Miss Bainbridge pulled up a chair beside her, shaking out her dove-grey skirts.

"It's not like you, I think," Miss Bainbridge said at last, thoughtfully, "to lie in so late. That's what I thought, at least. Imagine my surprise when I saw you rushing up to the house in the rain."

"It was you at the window, then," Lavinia said tightly. At least they weren't going to pretend to be friends, then. She was relieved. It was exhausting.

"It was me, yes," Miss Bainbridge sighed. "I hate all this rivalry, you know. I always imagined myself above those ladies who claw out the eyes of other women in pursuit of a man. I thought it rather demeaning."

"I couldn't agree more. And yet, here we are."

Miss Bainbridge shrugged. "I wish to be a duchess. The Duke is a fine man and will make a fine husband, I think. I believe I mentioned earlier that we have an understanding, and that was something which I had to organise myself. We women must take matters into our own hands, dear friend. Not an unfamiliar idea to you, I'm sure. Our world is not designed for women. Everything we want, we must carve out for ourselves. I think perhaps you understand, Miss Brookford."

"I am hardly a threat," Lavinia snapped. "My sister is perhaps more beautiful than either of us, but she is not interested in the duke. I am not more charming, or more accomplished, or more fascinating than you and I am certainly poorer."

"It is vulgar to talk of money, my dear."

"Vulgar, yes, but let's not pretend that the subject does not occupy everybody's mind, all the time."

Miss Bainbridge smiled. "Ah. That is where you are wrong. Those who *have* money do not feel the need to think about it very often. You betray your breeding, Miss Brookford."

Lavinia bit her lip. "Why are you here, Miss Bainbridge? Why are you speaking to me at all?"

Miss Bainbridge sighed. "I wanted to be open with you."

"I don't believe you've ever been open with anyone in your life."

The woman gave a genteel chuckle. "Goodness, my dear, put away your claws, won't you? I have never pretended to honesty, and I don't intend to start now. Tell me, how *did* you get that nasty stain on your hem? Not pacing the carpets in your bedroom, I warrant."

Lavinia clapped a hand over the stain on her skirt, rather guiltily, no doubt. It was too late, of course.

"I was walking," she lied, a little pleased with the smoothness with which she said it. Miss Bainbridge, naturally, was not fooled. She pursed her lips in a theatrical frown, tilting her head to one side.

"Is that *so*? Well, I heard quite a different story."

Lavinia closed her eyes momentarily. It was clear, then. Miss Bainbridge knew. The woman took her silence for an invitation to continue, and did so, with merciless clarity.

"You went for a ride this morning. Alone. And then the duke joined you, and you rode together. Also alone."

"The groom..."

"Was left behind," Miss Bainbridge interrupted curtly. "You were alone. It's a shocking circumstance, and one that would ruin you. If it were not for the stain it would leave on the duke's reputation, I should make the story known at once. I should have no scruples."

"Don't speak to me of your *scruples*," Lavinia snapped, anger boiling up inside her. Across the room, she saw Gillian's head lift, tuned in to her sister's voice.

"Keep your voice down," Miss Bainbridge hissed, as if reading her thoughts.

"You intend to expose me, do you not? Well, then, you ought to do it. Go on, then. Announce it right this moment. It's true, you can't tarnish me without affecting the duke, and I daresay your doting parents won't want you to marry a man with a stain. Just like you wouldn't want to wear a dress with a stain like mine. So, go on. I dare you, Miss Bainbridge."

Miss Bainbridge's face, always pale, was turning a mottled red. She clearly had not expected the bluff to be called.

"You are shameless," she hissed. "Riding alone, unchaperoned, and then walking into the duke's home looking like a blowsy plain woman. I should be ashamed if I were you."

"But you are not me, are you?"

Miss Bainbridge leaned closer; eyes narrowed. "I could drop a word in the dowager's ear. I might suggest that you are trying to *catch* her son, like the shameless flirt you are."

"If I am trying to secure his affections, then you are even worse than I," Lavinia responded staunchly. "You're getting rather desperate, my dear."

"He would never marry you," Miss Bainbridge spat. Her customary composure was deserting her, but Lavinia could not find it in herself to be triumphant. "Regardless of any *feelings* he might have, you are not the woman for him. You'll never be a duchess. He is informally engaged to *me*, do you hear? Betrothed! There will be an announcement soon, but for now, his honour will keep him by my side."

Lavinia flinched as if she'd been slapped. Her initial response was to call Miss Bainbridge a liar. She almost did, but then she looked straight into the woman's face and saw truth there.

"I see," Lavinia heard herself say, the words wrenched out of her.

Miss Bainbridge smiled tightly. "His pride will keep him cleaved to me if nothing else. You are not the woman for him."

Lavinia bit her lip, hard. "Perhaps I am not. But I should never want to marry a man who could not put aside his pride and his sense of station to marry the woman he loved. If he truly loved her, of course."

Miss Bainbridge blinked, seemingly taken aback. "How differently we feel," she remarked, voice sinking to a curious murmur. Now that the news was shared, the unofficial engagement on the cusp of becoming *official*, it seemed that a weight had lifted from her shoulders. She seemed more interested than angry now, eyeing Lavinia as if she were an animal in a cage. "Aren't you going to ask me whether I intend to speak to the dowager about you or not?"

Lavinia picked at her skirts. "Frankly, I could not care less. Speak to her, or don't. But if you have your say, I can assure you that I'll have mine, too."

Miss Bainbridge allowed herself a small smile at this, almost as if she were genuinely amused at Lavinia. It was infuriating, and Lavinia had to swallow down the desire to slap the wretched woman across the face.

Abruptly, a shadow fell across them, making both women jump. Gillian stood there, her thin slippers and soft gown making no sound as they slid across the carpet.

How much did she hear? Lavinia thought, with a pang of worry. This was not Gillian's concern. She should not be worrying about her sister being blackmailed by Miss Bainbridge, of all people.

"Lavinia," she said, her voice a trifle unsteady, "I'm feeling a little tired. Would you take me upstairs to rest before we go to the Assembly rooms, please?"

Lavinia frowned, taking in her sister's bright eyes and smooth face.

The little clever girl isn't tired at all, she thought, biting back a smile. *She's giving me an excuse to leave.*

She only nodded, getting to her feet. "Of course, Gillian. Come, take my arm."

Gillian hesitated, glancing down at Miss Bainbridge.

"Are you quite well, Miss Bainbridge?"

The woman flinched, glancing warily up at Gillian. "Of course."

"Oh. It's just that you look rather tired and unwell. You are looking remarkably sallow today. Perhaps you ought to rest a little, too. I find a short lie-down before an activity remarkably refreshing."

With that, Gillian turned on her heel, head high, dragging Lavinia behind her.

"Wretched woman," Lavinia heard her sister say under her breath. "How dare she speak to you like that?"

The last thing Lavinia saw before the door closed behind them, shutting them safely out into the hall, was Miss Bainbridge furtively lifting a hand to her cheeks, pinching them to bring colour into them.

The two sisters burst into laughter.

Chapter Twenty-One

I'm doing it. I'm truly doing it.
Father was wrong. I'm not a coward. I never was.

These were the thoughts that shot through William's mind as he rode, terror and exhilaration gripping him in equal measure. The mare moved easily and smoothly, responding at once to his tiniest touch of the reins. He knew, of course, that the horse was simply following its companion, but it did him good to imagine himself in control of the situation.

Miss Brookford had ridden well, he remembered that much. The woman was a natural horse rider, she and her horse moving as one. Now that it was over and half a day had passed, however, his ride almost seemed like a dream.

Not a dream, though. I rode a horse for the first time since father's death. I wasn't thrown, I wasn't injured in any way, and nor was anybody else. I did it.

The rain continued, heavy as ever, as he dressed absently. They were all going to the Assembly Rooms at the Pump Room tonight, where all of Bath Society gathered as often as they could. There would be supper, and music, and dancing, of course. The gentlemen were less interested in the Assembly Rooms, and there was a great deal of worry that the rain would not ease up in time for the hunting outing the next day.

William had not planned to hunt, of course, but after his ride only that morning, he felt... well, he wished to repeat the process. He wanted to ride again. An image of the stallion popped into his mind, and he shifted uneasily.

Not that creature, of course.

That reminded him, Miss Brookford had not yet chosen a name for the horse. Perhaps she did not believe he was serious when he told her she could choose. Biting his lip, he nodded at his valet, who was making the finishing touches on his cravat.

"That'll do, thank you. Don't wait up for me, of course. It's likely to be a late night."

The valet bowed. "Of course, your Grace. I do hope you enjoy yourself."

He smiled absently. "Oh, I'm sure I shall. I hope so, at the very least."

The man withdrew, leaving William staring at his reflection, gathering his thoughts.

I must tell her tonight. She deserves to know the truth.

No, it was too soon. William's apology was still raw, and he still flinched over his own curtness to her.

I'll dance with her tonight.

The thought of seeing Lavinia again filled his chest with warmth and anticipation, with a fair dollop of anxiety in the mix, too.

He could already hear the chatter and laughter drifting up from downstairs, with some guests already prepared to go, calling their carriages and making plans to meet up with each other once they reached the Assembly rooms. He closed his eyes.

Time to go.

***

William travelled with his two brothers and their respective wives, crammed in between poor Abigail and Eleanor, Alexander and Henry arguing about something in the opposite carriage seat. He smiled to himself, watching the dark landscape flit past.

Am I... am I excited over this outing? If I am, it's only because of her.

The ride, it seemed, had changed everything. It seemed ludicrous that he had ever seriously considered Miss Bainbridge. She was perfect for the role of duchess, indeed, but somehow the idea of marrying her was hollow.

"William?" Abigail said, her gentle voice cutting into his thoughts. "You seem preoccupied. Is everything well?"

"Hm? Oh, yes, I'm quite well. I think I'm just looking forward to the party."

Abigail smiled, and Henry gave a splutter of laughter across the carriage.

"You? Looking forward to something social? That can't possibly be right."

"Don't be cruel, you silly man," Eleanor responded, nudging her husband's knee with her foot. "I wonder who William is more eager to see – Miss Bainbridge, or Miss Brookford?"

The two brothers gave a whoop of laughter at that, and William allowed himself a small smile. He was with family, after all. One had to endure a little teasing.

"You're all wretched," he remarked, "and none of you deserve to know."

There was more hooting and laughter at that, and they kept jesting with each other all the way to the Assembly Rooms.

The grand building was all lit up from the inside-out, lights glowing from the windows. Carriages lined up outside, with finely dressed ladies and gentlemen climbing out, hats and bonnets crammed onto their heads to fend off the light, misting rain. The heavy showers of earlier had faded away, leaving only the promise of a clear night, fresh air, and a fine day tomorrow.

The Willenshires' carriage rumbled up next, and the five of them untangled themselves from each other and went hurrying up the steps. The heat hit William before they reached the door, and he felt a powerful wave of anxiety.

She would be here. He hadn't seen Lavinia since that morning, and nerves twanged at his gut. He hadn't even decided what he would say to her, only that it was time to come clean. He would tell her about the locket, about all of it. He would tell her about his feelings, about his father's will, about his own fears. Perhaps she didn't want to be a duchess. Sensible women generally didn't – it was a great deal of work and a lot of scrutiny, for surprisingly little reward.

Stop thinking of her. Miss Bainbridge is your betrothed, not Miss Brookford.

He stepped into the Assembly rooms proper, blinking in the glare of countless candelabras.

The place was packed full of ladies and gentlemen, all of them talking at once, loud enough to drown out the music.

And then he saw her.

Lavinia was wearing a deep blue dress, the same dress she'd worn all those months ago when they first met. It seemed like an eternity ago now.

His brothers and sisters-in-law filtered away, spotting acquaintances in the crowd, leaving William to stand alone. He felt oddly breathless.

Lavinia's gaze met him and stayed fixed on him.

William had read in books before how a pair of people might see each other across the room, lose their breath, and feel as though nothing and no one mattered but each other. He had always regarded it as feeble nonsense, trivialities that no sensible person could ever consider with gravity.

Well, he felt a little different now.

With a start, he realized that Lavinia was coming towards him, clutching the sides of her gown with something that could have been anxiety.

"Hello, your Grace," she said, smiling nervously and dropping a curtsey. "I was starting to think you might not come."

"Well, I'm... I'm here now," he managed. Weak stuff. He ought to do better than that. "Is your dance card full?"

She glanced down at the card hanging from her wrist and pulled a face. He wanted to laugh aloud. Ladies weren't meant to pull faces.

"About half-full, I'd say. I'm not used to being in demand, you know."

He chuckled, feeling some of his tension relax. "I was hoping you would dance with me. Do you have a partner for this next set? I can hear that the dancing has already begun."

She smiled tentatively up at him, her expression soft, hopeful, and so warm that it made him want to grin like a madman.

I love her. How could I have ever thought I felt differently?

"I should love to dance with you, your Grace."

He grimaced. "I hate being called that. It always reminds me of my father. My name is William."

She bit her lip. "It's not proper. If anyone overheard..."

"I apologise, I shouldn't have suggested it."

"No, it isn't your fault. It's theirs, really," she gestured at the room in general, her point fairly clear. "I can call you William in my head, I suppose."

He had to smile at that. "Well, if we intend to dance for this set, we ought to take our places now. What do you think?"

"I think that is an excellent idea, your Grace. Forgive me, *William*."

The dance slipped by faster than he could have imagined. It was some jig or other, and he found it remarkable that he didn't tread on her toes, or trip over his own feet, or anything like that. She kept looking up at him, a strange expression in her eyes, and he could feel his pulse pounding in his ears.

When the music ended, with a flourish almost drowned out by cheers and clapping, he blinked around, almost disoriented.

"I have something to tell you," he said aloud, before he could allow himself to think twice. "It's important."

She hadn't heard. Lavinia squinted up at him, cupping a hand around her ear. "I beg your pardon?"

He bit his lip. "Nothing. Let us get some refreshments."

I will tell her tonight, he decided. It made perfect sense. He had seen how her hand kept creeping up to the space at her collarbone, as if subconsciously reaching for a jewel that hung there. He'd seen how she flinched when the item was not there, and how she dropped her hand, looking foolish. It had played out over and over again.

He knew, of course, how much the locket meant to her. Or rather, what it represented – a gift from her brother, his childhood picture kept inside. He had already kept it for too long. It was high time to return it.

It was high time, too, to tell her about his betrothal. She deserved to know. She did.

Lavinia followed him, her arm looped through his, as they pushed their way through the crowds towards the refreshment centre. He caught a glimpse of Mr. Bainbridge, who tossed his head and turned his back.

William blinked, surprised at the snub. But then, it was fairly odd that Miss Bainbridge had not tried to seek him out already. Perhaps she had finally given up. He felt a twinge of guilt at his own cowardice, but there was plenty of relief in there, too.

They reached the refreshment table, and he poured out a cup of punch for himself and for Lavinia. She drank it down in large, unladylike gulps, and he bit back a smile.

"Heavens, I'm exhausted already," she remarked, shaking her head and setting down the cup. "It hardly bodes well, does it? Exhausted after one dance."

"I must agree with you," he answered. "Dancing is tiring, however. How is your sister?"

"Gillian? Oh, she's fine. She's been storing up her strength for tonight and will either be dancing with Lord Langley or waiting to dance with him again." She chuckled, shaking her head again.

"His attentions have been marked. He seems a good sort of man, and Miss Gillian appears to like him."

"Yes, I think so. Forgive me, your Grace, but I think you said something earlier, which I did not quite understand? On the dance floor? It seemed important."

Anxiety tightened in William's chest. He gave a brief smile. "Yes, I believe there was something I wanted to discuss with you."

"Oh?"

He slipped his hand into his pocket, feeling for the muslin-wrapped parcel. It would be the easiest thing in the world to help her understand. He would take out the locket, unwrap it, and she would be reunited with her precious jewel once again. Reunited with her brother.

It wasn't there.

William blinked, feeling a bead of sweat make its way down the side of his temple. Whether it was because of anxiety or the heat of the room, he was not sure.

The locket was certainly not in his pocket. Panic surged through his mind, throwing up horrific visions of pickpockets, of accidents, of thieving servants, or even a malicious Miss Bainbridge. He calmed down a little once he recalled taking the parcel out of his pocket and laying it down on the desk in his study.

However, of course, that meant he had a new, pressing problem to solve. Lavinia was looking up at him, mildly curious.

"Are you quite alright?" she asked, tilting her head. "You've gone as white as a sheet."

He laughed awkwardly. "Have I? I'm surprised, as it's so hot in here it feels like all of the blood had rushed to my head."

She smiled slightly at his clumsy joke. "Do you need to sit down?"

"I'm not in such need *yet*." He removed his hand from his pocket, wondering if he dared try the others. Lavinia would notice at once that he was looking for something, and then he would have to make excuses, or worse, tell a frank lie. Somehow, the truth did not seem possible.

The whole story seemed weak and almost unbelievable, here in the heat and noise of the Assembly Rooms. He would have to shout to be heard, telling her how he had her precious locket and had chosen not to return it. He would have to explain, of course, but not here. Here was not the right place to talk about anything serious, or anything personal, or anything that required straightforward talk and carefully thought-out answers.

"What did you want to say, then?" Lavinia said at last, making William jump.

No, they couldn't possibly discuss it here. But Lavinia was looking up at him curiously, waiting for a response.

He cleared his throat, avoiding her eye. "Do you know, I truly can't remember. I'm sure it'll come to me."

She smiled wryly. "I'm sure."

"I... did you want to dance again? The next set is starting soon, I think."

She smiled gently. "We can't dance twice in a row, can we? The world will think that we're betrothed."

He cleared his throat, shifting his weight awkwardly.

What is wrong with me? I'm acting like a fool!

It was just typical that he would forget to the put the locket in his pocket at the time he wanted it. When had it stopped being so important to him to carry the locket around? It wasn't his. It never had been his. Could it be that now Lavinia was here, and by seeing her so regularly, it somehow... somehow did not matter?

No, that was ridiculous. Truly ridiculous. It was just a locket.

"No, no, of course not," he said, smiling nervously. "I beg your pardon. I don't know what's wrong with me tonight. I would like to speak to you soon, though. Tomorrow, perhaps?"

Her eyes widened. "If you like."

He nodded abruptly. "We can't discuss it here."

"As you wish."

A silence descended between them, the noise of the Assembly rooms hemming in. Lavinia broke the quiet first.

"Shall we partake in more of the punch? I find myself quite parched."

"Yes," he said firmly. "That is a very good idea."

Chapter Twenty-Two

Lavinia woke lazily, stretching her arms above her head. She'd slept deeply, her dreams full of dancing and laughter and *him*.

He loves me, she thought, head spinning. *He must love me, to speak to me like that, to dance with me so often.*

She kept thinking about their ride together, the panic on his face when the horse had first broken into a rolling walk, and the way his composure gradually returned, colour coming back into his cheeks. A wave of powerful affection swept through her, so intense it made her shiver.

What was he going to tell me? He asked to speak to me in private. Could it be a proposal?

That idea seemed so ludicrous she almost rejected it at once. A man like the duke proposing to her was... well, almost beyond considering.

I could think of him as William *now, though,* she thought, allowing herself a small smile. She had no idea whether the private conversation he wanted would end in a proposal, or if it was just some other matter. Perhaps he intended to marry Miss Bainbridge after all and wanted to warn her.

And then, with a chilling sensation, she recalled what Miss Bainbridge had said about the betrothal.

Even so, that notion now possessed no sting. Miss Bainbridge had been remarkably subdued at the Assembly Rooms, sticking with her parents and talking to few people. She had not danced with the duke at all and had gone home early in the evening. Lavinia had managed to feel a pang of pity for her. What woman would hold a man to an engagement that he clearly didn't want? It wasn't her fault, after all.

Well, perhaps some of it was, but not all.

Outside, sunlight streamed into the room. It was pale, early-morning light. The hunting outing was still scheduled for today, but considering the late night everybody had had, it was considered likely that they wouldn't get started until late morning at least. She had time for a walk, or perhaps a short ride on Stepper. Lavinia was not, of course, going to go hunting. Not because she was a lady, but because she simply didn't enjoy chasing down and killing animals.

Yawning, she rolled out of bed, dressing quickly. Last night, Lord Langley had shown such special attention to Gillian that their mother had gloated about the wedding for hours afterwards. There'd been no proposal, of course, not yet, but it was fairly certain that there *would* be one.

Dressed in an old gown, with a shawl to stave off the morning chill and her trusty riding boots, Lavinia tiptoed through the quiet house and out into the morning air.

It was shaping up to be a fine day. No rain today, just clear skies and brisk sunlight. The air was sharply cold, but that wasn't the worst thing for a hunting outing. Dew and patches of frost still littered the fields, and in places, thick white fog clung to the ground. The courtyard was still and quiet. Peaceful, just the way Lavinia liked it. She breathed deeply as she walked, tipping back her head to look up at the sky.

It was going to be a near perfect ride.

She approached the stable door, which was partially ajar, and extended her hand to fling it open. Voices from inside made her hesitate.

Familiar voices.

"I don't know what to do, Timothy. I've gotten myself into quite a mess."

Prickles ran down her spine. That was the duke's voice. *William's* voice.

Timothy gave a heavy sigh. She hadn't spent much time with Timothy Rutherford, Katherine's husband, but he was a pleasant, well-liked man who seemed reserved around his vivacious wife and talkative in-laws. He had been William's friend for many years before his marriage to Katherine, she recalled.

"You'll have to be honest, Will. You must see that."

"Of course I do, it's just... oh, I've left it too long. How could I go about it now? Lavinia will never forgive me."

She flinched at the sound of her own name. Heart hammering, Lavinia inched closer, peering through the crack in the door. At the back of her mind, she seemed to recall that eavesdropping rarely worked out well for the eavesdropper, but she simply couldn't help herself.

Inside the stables, she saw William standing in front of one of the horse stalls. It contained the mild-tempered mare he'd ridden before, who was placidly eating pieces of carrot from his palm. Timothy Rutherford stood nearby, arms folded tight, leaning against the wall. He looked serious, a frown tightening up his forehead.

"Pray, I advise you to see to it without further ado," Timothy remarked. "To postpone will serve you naught. You should know that the Bainbridges are highly offended, and nothing good will come from *that*. Besides, the Brookfords now have raised hopes. If you intend to disappoint them, then..."

"Oh, stop it, Timothy. I told you, my decision is made. I've chosen my duchess."

She sucked in a breath, immediately clapping a hand over her mouth in case she was overheard.

He's chosen his duchess? What does that mean? Has she chosen me? Could it be me?

"I accepted Miss Bainbridge's offer. We are betrothed. There is nothing I can do about it."

Lavinia's heart plunged into her stomach.

We are betrothed. We are betrothed.

What a fool I've been, she thought, pressing a hand over her mouth. William continued, as if he had not inadvertently destroyed Lavinia's hopes.

"The issue," William said, passing a hand over his face, "is the locket."

Locket.

The word seemed to explode in Lavinia's mind like a cannonball. Almost unconsciously, her hand crept up to her collarbone, to the hollow at the base of her throat where Hugh's locket and his picture had sat for years and years. As always, her fingers touched only empty skin.

"Are you *sure* that it's hers?" Timothy asked. "Silver lockets are fairly common in this part of the world."

William nodded tightly. "It's hers. The private investigator confirmed it. The locket is Lavinia's, and the picture is of her brother. It took him quite a while to track her down, I can tell you. She wasn't an easy woman to find. But find her he did, and he assured me that it does belong to her. She dropped it at the first party we ever met. The clasp broke. I often wish that I'd just handed it over to the hostess, but of course it's too late now. I shouldn't have waited so long."

The door stood ajar before Lavinia was aware of it, flung open to strike against the wall and then rebound. Both men nearly leapt out of their skin, spinning around to face her. The colour drained from William's face. He dropped his handful of carrots onto the straw-covered floor, and the mare gave a huff of annoyance.

"Lavinia," he gasped. "I mean, I mean, Miss Brookford. I had no idea you were..."

"No idea I was outside?" she said, her own voice seeming to come from far away. Blood pounded in her ears.

"What did you hear, Miss Brookford?" Timothy asked uneasily, glancing at William. "I think you may have misunderstood..."

"Misunderstood what? That all of this, your... your *pursuit* of me, if I can call it that, was all in aid of returning a locket? You were engaged all along, weren't you? Miss Bainbridge tried to warn me, but I scarcely believed her. Was it all just a grand joke, something fun for a rich, idle young man to entertain himself with?"

William shook his head, taking a step forward. "Miss Brookford... *Lavinia*. That is not what I meant at all. Picking up your locket was an accident, and I had no idea who it belonged to, and..."

"And so you hired a *private investigator* to find me," she interrupted bitterly. "What else did he tell you, I wonder? Did he mention that I was a ridiculous spinster? That my family is desperate to marry off my pretty younger sister, as if we were auctioning her off? I'm sure he made mention of our dire financial situation. Is... is that why we were invited here?"

"No," he said firmly, but she shook her head, barely listening. "Miss Brookford, please. Perhaps I have handled matters badly, but I only ever intended to return the locket to you. Its value was clear, and..."

"Value? What does a man like you know about *value*? I'm sure you value Miss Bainbridge and her fortune. Oh, how foolish I've been. I wonder if you've both been planning it all out. She, at least, seemed to have some pity for me. How long have you been watching me, *your Grace*?"

William glanced desperately at his friend. Timothy drew in a breath and took a step towards her.

"Miss Brookford, *please*..."

"I've heard enough," she interrupted. Tears were pricking at her eyes, silly baby tears which were about to fall at any moment and make her look like a fool, like a simple minded young lady who let her hopes outpace rational thought.

Did I really think a man like him would marry a woman like me?

"Give me my locket," she said at last, voice wobbling.

William bit his lip. "I... I don't have it with me, I am so sorry. I'll fetch it at once, I..."

"Don't bother."

She turned on her heel and strode out of the stables. She heard the men begin to follow her, both calling out, and she broke into a run, hauling her skirts up above her ankles.

Whether they ran after her or not, Lavinia had no idea. Her vision blurred, eyes stinging with tears, and she simply concentrated on putting one foot in front of the other.

Racing into the house, she nearly collided with a footman, who gave a yelp of surprise and shouted something after her. She kept going, crossing the foyer and stumbling up the stairs. Blindly, she reached the door to her room, threw herself inside, and burst into hot, noisy tears.

***

"Lavinia? Lavvy, please open the door. It's me, Lavinia."

Lavinia sniffed, wiping her swollen eyes with the back of her hand. "Go away, Gillian. You'll miss the hunt. It must be starting soon."

She heard a rustling noise on the other side of the door, which was probably Gillian sinking down into a sitting position, right out in the hall.

"I don't want to go hunting. Mama and Papa weren't going, and you know how I hate to hunt. Please, tell me what's wrong."

"I can't. It's too humiliating."

"I am your sister, Lavinia. What is so terrible that you can't tell me? The Duke came to ask for you, you know. Mama made up some excuse, but it's clear that something is amiss. Why won't you *talk* to me?"

Lavinia drew in a deep breath, squeezing her eyes closed.

"I've been a simpleton, Gillian. I've been such a simpleton."

There was a long silence on the other side of the door. Then Gillian let out a long, tired sigh.

"Let me in, Lavinia. Please."

After another lengthy pause, Lavinia shuffled to one side, reaching up to unlock the bedroom door. Gillian came crawling in, closing the door after her.

For a while, the two sisters sat side by side in silence.

Lavinia spoke first.

She started right at the beginning, with the night she met William, Duke of Dunleigh, for the first time, discovering later that her precious necklace was gone. Gillian's face tightened at the mention of Hugh, but she said nothing, letting Lavinia continue.

Lavinia talked about her hopes and dreams, the feelings that had gradually grown up inside her when she was around the duke. She talked about the things Miss Bainbridge had said, the threats she had made, and Gillian did not look particularly surprised to hear this.

Her sister's face turned dark and angry when she talked about what she had heard at the stables.

"He is betrothed? Since our arrival at the house? Oh, Lavinia, I am so terribly sorry, my darling girl. He hired a man to *investigate* you?" she gasped. "Oh, that is foolish of him, Lavinia. There was still time for him to return the locket to the hostess. You went back to ask about it, didn't you? And… and I do not understand why he kept the locket for such a long time. It makes no sense to me."

"Nor to me," Lavinia admitted, wiping her eyes. Gillian fumbled in her pocket, coming up with a delicate lace-edged handkerchief with a *G* embroidered in the corner. Lavinia took it and blew her nose noisily.

"Would you like me to speak to him? I could ask for your locket back."

"No," Lavinia said, more loudly than she had intended. "No, Gillian. Let it be. I suppose it serves me right for eavesdropping. Oh, Gilly, I assure you, this must be some grand jest, a scheme devised by Miss Bainbridge and him together. Do you believe I am losing my senses?"

Gillian was quiet for a long moment.

"No," she said at long last. "I don't think it's anything so complicated. Perhaps he simply did not take the locket as anything valuable. Perhaps he was bored and entertained himself by finding the owner. Perhaps he simply kept forgetting to return it."

She sniffled. "Perhaps. I have overstated my importance to him, then, haven't I?"

Gillian bit her lip and said nothing. There was nothing *to* say, after all.

"Was there ever a more naive young woman than me, eh?" Lavinia managed at last, smiling weakly. "Oh, Gillian, I wish I was home. I wish it with all of my heart."

"You can go home. We should tell Mama and Papa, and…"

Lavinia shook her head. "No, Gilly. They'd never agree, and I wouldn't ask it of them. Mama is having a good time for the first time in quite a while. She and the dowager are becoming firm friends. Papa is comfortable here, and I do think he's enjoying himself. And you… well, you have Lord Langley, don't you?"

Gillian blushed. "That's hardly relevant."

"It is relevant. We came here to make connections, did we not? Mama wants you married. *You* want to get married. What sort of sister would I be if I ruined it for us all because of some silly heartbreak of my own? I'm strong enough to manage."

"Yes, but you shouldn't have to," Gillian insisted. "What sort of sister would *I* be, if I could enjoy myself at a house party where you were so miserable?"

Reaching out, Gillian took her sister's hand, lacing their fingers together. Despite herself, Lavinia leaned sideways, sagging until she could rest her head on her sister's shoulder. Closing her eyes, she tried to think of nothing. Not of Miss Bainbridge, or Hugh, or the locket, or the mysterious, faceless private investigator that had been following her for goodness only knew how long.

Or of *him*.

She never wanted to think of him again. And yet, she was fairly sure she would not be able to think of anything else.

A strangled sob escaped from Lavinia's lips, no matter how hard she tried to swallow it down.

"Oh, Lavinia," Gillian whispered, voice breaking. "I can't bear this."

"Well, I can," Lavinia responded at once. "I can, and I should. It's no more than I deserve. What did I think would happen, setting my sights on a man like the duke? He was never for the likes of me."

"This isn't like you, Lavinia. You never speak so harshly of yourself."

Abruptly, Lavinia climbed to her feet, dragging her hand away from Gillian's. She paced up and down her room, still shrouded in gloom from the closed curtains. Somehow, she was sure that if she pulled back the curtains and let in the light, she would break down in tears again.

"Perhaps I needed a little more understanding," she said, half to herself. "I do think highly of myself. Too highly, perhaps. I am a *spinster*, and a penniless one. I have no great accomplishments, a fairly ordinary sort of beauty, and no powerful family to support me. I have nothing, really."

"Stop it, Lavinia."

"No, I need to say this. I am a fool, Gillian. I let myself believe that the duke could love somebody like me. Others tried to warn me. Miss Bainbridge, even, tried to save me the humiliation, but I would not listen. Oh, to think that I considered myself her *rival!*" she gave a peal of mirthless laughter. "I am so foolish. But I'm glad that this has happened, Gillian. Seeing oneself as one is truly might be painful, but it's better in the long run. Much better."

Gillian stared at her for a long moment, lips pressed together.

"We should leave," she said at last.

"I won't ask Mama and Papa to take us home."

Gillian let out a long, slow breath. "Very well. Then I shall ask them."

And before Lavinia could say or do a thing, Gillian turned on her heel and hurried out of the room.

Chapter Twenty-Three

William felt as though his feet were rooted to the ground. Timothy had gone rushing to the door of the stables, staring across the courtyard after her. He paused in the doorway, glancing back at William.

"You should go after her. Tell her it was a misunderstanding. You need to *explain*, William."

"Explain what?" His lips felt numb. "It was all true. I did hire an investigator to find her. I did keep her locket for longer than I should. I don't have anything to say to that. It's true. I can't lie."

Timothy began to look exasperated. "Tell her that you love her, you utter fool."

William flinched. "I can't. I couldn't. How can I, after all that?"

His friend came towards him, gripping his shoulders. "Look at me. Look at me, Will! You can't be a coward. Not when it comes to love. Take it from somebody who almost lost everything. You *must* act."

"I'm not a coward."

"Then *do* something. Go after her. Tell her you'll break your betrothal off with Miss Bainbridge."

"I can't."

"You must! It is unfair to Miss Bainbridge – you *do not love her* – and it is unfair to yourself."

"It's dishonourable."

Timothy growled. "Dishonourable! I hate that word. Are you truly going to condemn yourself to a lifetime of misery because of one small mistake? If you tell Miss Brookford that you made a mistake, that you intend to end things with Miss Bainbridge, then perhaps she will think differently of you."

Biting his lip, William glanced across the courtyard. Lavinia had her head down, and was running as fast as she could. She had almost reached the steps.

He squeezed his eyes closed.

"No."

"*William...*"

"Not *yet*. She needs time to calm down."

Timothy made an exasperated noise. "You've said that a great deal lately, William *Not yet*. Be careful that *not yet* does not become never."

William said nothing in response to this. Really, there was nothing *to* say.

***

Most of the guests had left for the hunt. William had made an excuse and taken himself to the privacy of his study. Today, he wasn't even pretending to do work. He stared into space, fingers drumming out a rhythm on the desk.

Timothy is right. I must speak to her.

I doubt she wants to speak to me at the moment. I'd be turned away.

What if she tells her family?

What have I done?

What if she won't forgive me?

What if I can't forgive myself?

With a groan, he dropped his head into his hands, fingers dishevelling his hair.

I don't know what to do.

A brusque tap on the door made him jerk upright. He blinked, mentally reviewing who might still be in the house.

He was fairly certain that Lavinia was still here, but his siblings and their respective spouses had all gone out. Perhaps Timothy had told Katherine about what had happened, and she was here to lecture him.

Richly deserved, I think. Only one way to find out.

"Enter," he said, hating how tremulous his voice sounded.

The door opened. Miss Bainbridge entered. Alone.

William flinched, eyes widening, and made to get up from the desk.

"Don't fret, my maid is right outside the door," Miss Bainbridge said wearily, pushing open the door a little further to show the maid in question. "I am not here to entrap you. May I sit?"

He cleared his throat, gesturing to a chair. She sat, carefully adjusting her skirts. After an awkward moment, he sank down too, clearing his throat.

"I thought you had gone out," he said at last, when the silence began to stretch on.

She shrugged. "I meant to go out, but I have no taste for hunting. I thought I would stay, and once I discovered that you were here, I thought we could talk, you and I."

He swallowed hard, glancing over at her.

Miss Bainbridge did not look well. She was paler than usual, with dark circles under her eyes. Her hair was as neatly arranged as ever, and her dress impeccable, but there was something missing about it all. A spark, perhaps.

"I believe that I owe you an apology," William heard himself say. "Directly or indirectly, I have made you believe that I was agreeable to... to the union you suggested. Which I accepted. I should not have accepted."

"To our marriage, you mean," she said bluntly, and then gave a tired smile at the shock on his face. "Come, your

Grace, let's be honest, shall we? I do like to be forthright in these matters."

He cleared his throat. "Yes, I suppose you are right. I... I did not know my own mind, and I should have been clear with you on that point. Darting between decisions was an ungentlemanly thing for me to do. I am sorry. But it matters not. I entered into an agreement with you, and I must stick to it, I know that now. Going forward, I will be a better man, and strive to... to make you happy."

She eyed him for a long moment, fingers drumming on the arm of her chair.

"I had made up my mind to marry you," she said at last. "I came here to have one last try, to convince you that we would make an excellent Duke and Duchess together."

He glanced down. "I think you would make an admirable duchess, Miss Bainbridge. You would do a far better job than I am doing as a duke. You are clever, logical, straightforward, and hardworking. You are a fine woman, and you deserve better than... than this," he made a vague gesture which he hoped encompassed all of what had gone on between them. She gave him a wry smile.

"How kind. I sense that you are about to add a *but*, though. So let me hear it."

He closed his eyes. "I am in love with Miss Brookford."

She gave a long, slow exhale. "Yes. Yes, I thought you were. It makes sense, I suppose. She has a... a vibrancy that I do not. Of course, I have money, a great deal of it, and breeding, which *she* does not, but that is neither here nor there."

"I ought to have been forthright with you," he repeated, forcing himself to meet her eye. "I... I did not expect to fall in love. I did not plan for it. Frankly, I intended to keep my heart clear of the marriage business altogether, as I thought that using only my head would make for a better decision. We discussed this, I know."

"I am inclined to agree."

"And indeed, here I am," he shrugged tiredly. "I love her. My heart is gone, and I cannot take it back."

Miss Bainbridge lifted her eyebrows. "She has refused you? What a surprise. I rather thought she was fond of you, too. At the very least, yours is an offer she should not pass up."

"No, no, I haven't asked her. How could I? You and I are... ahem. I would never make a proposal of marriage to a woman while I was engaged to another. To you, in point of fact."

She eyed him with those cool, beady eyes, waiting for him to finish, as if she knew it all already. "I have upset her quite badly," he finished at last. "Hardly surprising, considering my behaviour over the past weeks."

"Well, whatever it is, I'm sure you can smooth it over," Miss Bainbridge remarked, lifting an eyebrow. "A little honesty, a few sincere apologies are all it will take, yes?"

"I... I don't know."

Almost without thinking about it, William reached for the small, muslin-wrapped parcel on the desk. He hadn't taken the locket out to look at it for quite a while. Odd, considering how important the trinket had become to him recently.

"You won't know until you try," she said, offering what might have been a smile. "I bear you no ill will, your Grace. I'm not even angry at Miss Brookford. I *was* angry at her, I think, but perhaps you and I would not have been so ideally suited after all."

William blinked, glancing up. What was she talking about? They were betrothed. They were committed to each other. He had told her that he would engage into matrimony with her.

"I take my promises seriously. I will try my best to make you happy, Miss Bainbridge."

She gave a wry smile. "Bless you, your Grace, but I don't leave my happiness in the hands of others. I choose for myself whether to be happy or not."

He frowned. "I don't understand."

Miss Bainbridge suddenly looked very tired. "I release you from our betrothal, William. Such as it was, at least. If you wish to pursue Miss Brookford, you are free to do so."

"I... I don't know what to say," he stammered.

She chuckled. "There is nothing *to* say. I am simply informing you of this change in circumstances."

Abruptly, she rose to her feet, extending a hand. It took him a second or two to bounce to his feet as well, and he realised that she was not holding out her hand for him to take. She held it with the palm to one side, fingers straight. She was inviting a handshake, frank and open.

After only an instant's hesitation, he took it. It was like a huge weight had lifted off his shoulders. He felt almost shaky.

"I wish you all the best, Miss Bainbridge. I wish you might find love, as I have. I hope you'll manage it a little better than I have done."

She chuckled, reaching up to adjust her spectacles. "Perhaps I shall, perhaps I shall not. I hope we'll meet again, your Grace. I look forward to meeting your duchess under better circumstances."

He could only manage a smile in response. She dropped his hand, offered him a wry smile, and turned to leave.

William was left standing behind his desk, hands hanging by his side, listening to Miss Bainbridge's footsteps retreat, her maid scuttling behind.

He was still standing there like a statue when the butler came bursting in, out of breath.

"Your Grace, I am terribly sorry to interrupt you, I just... well, I thought you should know, seeing as everybody is out of the house, including her Grace the Dowager." The man was panting, sweat beading on his forehead, and it was fairly clear he'd run at least from one side of the house to another.

That's not like him, William thought, a sense of unease sparking in his chest.

"What's the matter?"

"It is the Brookford family," the butler said, regaining his breath. "I am *quite* sure that her Grace, the Dowager, is unaware of this, and they would not agree to wait even an hour longer! Her Grace will be quite upset, I fear. There'll be a great deal of talk about this, too. They would *not* be reasoned with. Their minds were quite made up."

"What are you talking about?" William felt the first throbs of a headache at his temples. "I don't understand."

The butler drew in a breath. "The Brookford family has packed up their things and left about ten minutes ago."

There was a moment of silence.

"I beg your pardon," William said at last. "You mean they have left, without warning or announcing it? Is there a note?"

The butler shook his head. "There was something of a kerfuffle this morning, I believe. I only heard of it half an hour ago, when the Brookford carriage was summoned. Their things were already half loaded by the time I arrived. I tried to get to the bottom of it, but Lord Brennon was remarkably uncooperative. He only said that he believed *you*, your Grace, would know the reason."

William swallowed hard, a lump forming in his throat.

He's right. I do know the reason. I shamed Lavinia Brookford, I hurt her more than I had ever intended to do, and now her family are leaving my home.

"Is... are all of them going?" he managed at last.

The butler sighed. "*Gone*, your Grace. All four of them. I watched the carriage move away. I thought, mistakenly, that *you* had gone out with the hunt, your Grace, or I would have told you at once. Of course, they cannot be *obliged* to stay, but..." he bit his lip. "There'll be a great deal of talk about this, your Grace. The nastiest rumours are started over things as silly as this. I cannot imagine what might have happened to offend the family, but..."

"I must go down to the stables," William said shakily, snatching up the locket from the table.

He left the study, sprinting down the hallway. The butler followed him, the poor man puffing and panting as he went. William felt a pang of sympathy, but really, there was no time to waste.

He went straight to the Brookfords' rooms. They were, as the butler had promised, empty, an odd sort of *deserted* feeling hanging in the air.

There was no note, nothing at all, not even a folded slip of paper left out on the chest of drawers.

William stood in the middle of one of the bedchambers, his breath coming hard, heart pounding.

What have I done?

Timothy warned me. Or tried to, at least. He told me that not yet *might easily become* never. *And now, my chance has slipped away.*

No. Not quite. It has nearly *slipped away. And that's not the same thing at all.*

"I'll need a horse," William said at last. The butler who had arrived puffing after him, flinched.

"A... a horse, your Grace?"

"Yes. There's a nice mare in the stables called Cinnamon. Saddle her up. I shall ride out after them."

The butler cleared his throat awkwardly. "There... there aren't any horses, your Grace. Not riding ones."

William rounded on him. "What did you say?"

The poor man shrank back. "The hunt, your Grace! Just about every horse in the stables has been taken out! I might be able to find a few horses from the farmlands to hire, and we could strap them up to one of the carriages, and..."

"No, no, that'll take too long. They've got a long enough head start. I'll never catch them in a carriage, or on some staid old carthorse." William dropped his head into his hands, giving a muffled groan. "Are there *no* horses at *all* in my stables?"

There was a long, pregnant pause.

"Well," the butler began carefully. "There is one horse."

William lifted his head. "Oh?"

The butler met his eye pointedly. "*A particular* horse, your Grace. The one that you said nobody was to ride. The... the horse that belonged to the late duke. The one that killed him."

William swallowed hard, fear drying up his throat. He glanced down at the driveway, which he could see clearly from the window.

Ten minutes. They've been gone for ten minutes. If I don't leave soon, I won't catch them.

He squeezed his eyes closed.

"Saddle him up."

The butler actually staggered backwards. "Your Grace?"

"You heard me. Saddle up that horse. Make haste, there's no time to lose."

Chapter Twenty-Four

There was absolute silence inside the Brookfords' carriage. Nobody looked at anybody else.

Lavinia was sitting beside her father. At the beginning of the journey, he'd thrown a few sympathetic looks her way. She hadn't been able to bring herself to look back.

He knew, of course. They all did. Gillian had stridden right over to their parents' room, gone into the small, attached parlour area, and explained the whole situation.

The reaction from Lady Brennon was exactly what Lavinia had expected.

"Don't be a simpleton, Gillian! Of course we cannot leave! I am sorry that Lavinia has been so disappointed over the duke, but after all, a duke was quite far from her reach, I think. What about *Lord Langley*?"

Lavinia, who had followed out of instinct rather than any real desire to hear what was being discussed, saw the way Gillian's face paled at the mention of Lord Langley. There was a flicker of anguish on her face, quickly smoothed away.

"If Lord Langley likes me as much as I think he does, he will write to me," Gillian had responded, as calm as she could.

Lavinia bit her lip. That was not necessarily true. Of course, Lord Langley *may* prove to be the sort of man who, once his heart had been touched by love, he would not quickly forget.

In Lavinia's opinion, however, gentlemen were more fickle than that. Men tended to forget rather quickly, once the lady of their affections was out from under their eye. Lord Langley might prove to be such a man, and then what of Gillian's heart?

An argument naturally broke out, between Gillian and Lady Brennon. It wasn't like Gillian to have such strong opinions about anything, and certainly not to stand up to her mother in such a fearsome way.

Lavinia lingered by the doorway and said nothing. When she glanced over at Lord Brennon, she found that he was already looking at her, his expression unreadable.

When a gap in the conversation came, he folded his newspaper away with slow, deliberate movements, and rose to his feet.

Lady Brennon turned pleadingly to her husband.

"Tell them, won't you? Tell them that we cannot throw away Gillian's prospects over an insult levelled at Lavinia."

He glanced between his daughters. "Gillian wants to leave, too."

"I do not care. We are going nowhere! Lavinia may ignore the duke if she likes, but I for one will not stand by and do nothing while..."

"We are leaving."

Lord Brennon uttered the three words slowly and carefully. Deliberately, almost. There was a brief silence after he spoke. Lady Brennon paled.

"What did you say?" she whispered.

"We are leaving," he repeated evenly. "Gillian wishes to go. Lavinia wishes to go, and I will not stay in a house where my daughter has been so insulted. If Hugh were here, he would say exactly the same. As for you, my dear, I will not drag you into the carriage. You may stay or go as you please. Girls, I suggest you begin packing."

It felt like a lifetime ago now. The packing had passed in a haze, with Lavinia crunching and crushing dresses almost beyond repair, shoving them deep down in the trunks. Lady

Brennon had come with them, of course, tight-lipped and visibly furious.

Green, leafy landscape rattled by them. Soon they would be out on the streets of Bath, weaving through the traffic, back out into the countryside.

I daresay we'll never come back here, Lavinia thought, her heart sinking more.

She wasn't sure whether she had truly absorbed what was going on, how entirely her prospects were destroyed. Their sudden departure would be all anybody would talk about for the rest of their stay. The Dowager's friendship with Lady Brennon was likely over. If they were lucky, a plausible excuse might be invented.

Lavinia did not feel particularly lucky at the moment. She leaned back against the carriage seat, resting her head and closing her eyes.

"We're ruined," Lady Brennon said bitterly, cutting into her thoughts.

"Stop it, Mama," Gillian said, with more sharpness in her voice than Lavinia had ever heard before.

It seems that my sweet, kindly little sister is finally starting to find her way and grow into herself, Lavinia thought. *All it took was all of my hopes and dreams to be dashed at one blow.*

And hers too, I imagine.

I never even got Hugh's locket back.

That felt like the hardest part of all. A lump formed in her throat, choking her and stinging her eyes with tears.

I could write to him when we get home. Request him to send over my locket. He knows how important it is to me, what Hugh meant to me. Surely, he would have a little pity, at least.

Miss Bainbridge might advise him to be kind. She can be a kind woman, I imagine, once she's won. Anybody can be generous in victory.

Deep down, however, Lavinia did not believe she could put pen to paper if she knew she were writing to the duke.

To William.

She could ask Gillian, perhaps, although Gillian had already done far too much on her behalf.

Lavinia bit her lip, praying that she would not disgrace herself with more tears in front of her family. She wasn't sure what was worse – the tangible sympathy on the faces of her father and sister, or the cold fury on her mother's.

Wouldn't it be funny if the carriage door opened up, right now, and I just tumbled out? Lavinia thought, hysterical laughter bubbling to the surface. *That would be pleasant. Just falling out into the ditches on either side of the road, perhaps knocking myself unconscious. Lord, what I wouldn't give to sleep for a while right now.*

Sleep seemed a long way off for her right now. Her father, naturally, was beginning to nod, eyes flickering.

Abruptly, without warning, nausea lurched in Lavinia's stomach, a sharp reminder that she had not eaten since last night.

"I feel sick," she murmured. Lady Brennon gave a snort.

"Well might you feel sick! I feel sick. All of us feel sick, on account of our prospects and hopes for the future dwindling into nothing! For my part, I am shocked and horrified to learn that..."

Lavinia tried to block out her mother's shrill, angry tones. Shifting towards the window, she focused on the scenery flashing by.

Are those horses' hooves I can hear? She thought faintly.

A black flash shot past the window, and Lavinia flinched back, gasping aloud.

"What is the matter with you now, Lavinia?" Lady Brennon snapped.

And then there was chaos.

A shout came from the coachman, and the entire carriage lurched forward and to the side, skidding to a painful halt. All of them were flung bodily from their seats.

In the painful silence that followed, Lavinia clearly heard a man shouting, a horse snorting, and the stamp of iron-clad hooves on hard-packed road.

"What's going on?" Lord Brennon quavered, reaching up to bang on the roof. "Coachman? What is it?"

"It's footpads," Lady Brennon gasped, clutching at Gillian's hands. "Oh, what have we done? What trouble are we in now? We are going to be robbed and then left dead on the side of the road!"

Lavinia tried to ignore her mother's panicked babbling, instead leaning forward and trying to catch glimpses of the conversation outside. The coachman sounded angry.

"Move aside, sir! What are you about?"

A muffled reply came, but the voice was familiar enough to make Lavinia suck in a breath. She glanced around the carriage to see if the others had realized just what was going on.

They hadn't. Lady Brennon was now wailing about being murdered and nobody ever finding their bodies – a change from her earlier fears, where their half-naked bodies would be deposited in a ditch besides the road – and she was clutching Gillian to her as if trying to protect her. Lavinia noticed with a wry smile that her mother did not seem to be particularly worried about *her*.

Lord Brennon looked a little less apprehensive. Apparently, he thought that footpads on a main road in Bath, in the middle of the day, was somewhat unlikely. He was shouting up to the coachman, and between the three of them, nobody was listening to Lavinia.

Biting back a curse of annoyance, she tried to peer out of the carriage, trying to get a glimpse of the horseman on the road, to confirm what she already knew.

It was no good. With a sigh of resignation, Lavinia unlatched the door and flung it open wide. Lady Brennon gave a shriek, and even Lord Brennon loudly demanded to know what Lavinia thought she was about to do.

She ignored them all.

The steps had not been put down, of course, leaving Lavinia to jump down the three feet to the ground. She landed nimbly, and turned back to close the door behind her, shutting off her view of her family's horrified and confused faces.

It was much quieter out here, away from the panicked chatter. She heard the coachman speak again.

"Get out of the way, sir. I won't tell you again."

"I can't," came the cool, clear, familiar voice. "I must speak to her."

Lavinia walked around to the front of the carriage.

"And here I am," she said, meeting his eye. "What do you want to say to me?"

Chapter Twenty-Five

William felt vaguely sick. He was sure that if he had anything for breakfast, he would likely have brought it up by now.

Riding the stallion was not at all like riding the mild-mannered Cinnamon. He had watched one of the grooms saddle up the horse, who watched him closely but made no move to bite or kick.

Perhaps it was just my father he wanted to bite and kick. I cannot say I blame him.

He hauled himself up into the saddle before he could think twice.

Pretend it is only Cinnamon. Just sweet, mild Cinnamon. Just Cin...

At that moment, the stallion lurched forward. He did not bother with a walk, or even a trot. He broke out into a gallop, leaving William with no time to cry out or do anything at all besides clutch onto the reins and lean forward.

He could hear various shouts coming from behind him. There was panicked yelling from the butler, and slightly more encouraging noises from the grooms. He wanted to turn around and look, but that seemed like a poor idea.

The stallion had galloped without slowing, heading down the correct road at just the tiniest touch of the reins. William forced himself to breathe, careful not to grip too hard with his legs in case the horse should imagine that he wanted it to go faster.

The scenery flew by, the road blurring underneath, and William gritted his teeth and held on.

It felt only minutes later that he saw the carriage. They had already almost passed it by the time he managed to tug on the reins, willing the stallion to slow down.

The horse skidded to a halt, its rump going down, and William managed to turn it around and face it towards the carriage.

The coachman hauled on the reins, face red, and the carriage lurched to a halt.

"What are you about?" the man yelled, waving his whip. "Get out of the way!"

"I can't," William responded, his voice shaking. "I need to speak to somebody inside the carriage."

"Certainly not. Move!"

Anger flared. "I cannot move. I need to speak to her!"

The shouted exchange went on, until William heard the slam of a carriage door.

Slowly, tentatively, Lavinia came towards him. She stared at him as if he'd grown two heads.

After a long pause, she glanced up at the coachman. "I'll have a word with him, Michael. If you don't mind."

The coachman sighed. "As you like, Miss Brookford. I'll check on the family inside the carriage, make sure everybody is quite alright."

Lavinia nodded without looking at him. The two of them kept their eyes fixed on the other as the coachman lumbered down from his post and went around the other side of the carriage.

Summoning his courage, William slid down from the stallion's back. His legs felt like jelly, and he didn't trust himself to go over to Lavinia just yet.

"You're riding Sapphire," she said, after a pause.

"Sapphire?"

She nodded at the stallion. "You said I could name him, didn't you?"

William paused, nodding. "I did. Lavinia, I'm here to apologise. And, before I say a single word, I must give you this."

He reached into his pocket with a shaking hand, holding out the locket. He saw her face tighten when she saw it. At once, she darted forward and snatched it out of his hand. He stepped back, letting her have a moment with the locket.

She stared down at the necklace, cupped in her palm, and stroked her thumb over the pendant. After a moment, she opened it up, and he saw her smile down at the picture inside.

"It's good to see you again, Hugh," she said, voice quiet. She closed up the pendant and slipped it carefully into her pocket.

"You might want to repair the clasp," William said, after a pause.

"I will. Why are you here, William?"

"Aside from the apology, and to return your locket?" He smiled wryly. "I let you walk away from the stables, Lavinia, because I believed that you needed time to cool down. My old friend, Timothy, told me to go after you, but I didn't listen. I wish I had."

She only looked at him, her expression unreadable. "And Miss Bainbridge? Your betrothed?"

He swallowed hard. "I have used Miss Bainbridge badly. She did not deserve any of this. She... She has given up, Lavinia. She visited me and released me from our betrothal. I'm not sure that I deserved her kindness, or any understanding at all."

Lavinia's shoulders lowered. "You… you made a mistake. Nobody would hold it against you."

He shook his head. "I did wrong. I know that. But the truth is, the simple truth is that I love you, Lavinia. You. Not Miss Bainbridge. I wanted to marry her because she seemed perfectly suitable, but I know now that it would never work. I would not make her happy, and I would not make myself happy. I'm glad that she saw that in the end, and that I saw it, too. I want to marry you, Lavinia Brookford."

She flinched, swallowing hard. "I am a spinster."

"I am older than you."

"I have no money."

He breathed in. "Neither do I."

She raised her eyebrows. "Forgive me if I don't entirely believe you."

"The truth is…" he steeled himself and continued. "My father left a singular type of will. None of us can inherit our share of the Willenshire fortune until we marry. We have one year from the reading of the will to qualify."

She sucked in a breath. "Truly? How awful for you all."

He shrugged. "My siblings are happy. They have married people they loved. For me, marriage was a necessity. The Duke of Dunleigh can't be penniless, after all. I never for a moment imagined that I would fall in love. My father never did. I thought Miss Bainbridge would suit, and so did she, I think. And then I met you."

Lavinia swallowed. "I see."

"I love you, Lavinia. I loved you from the moment we first met, when I did not even know your name. Perhaps that is why I held onto the locket, and why I tried so hard to find you and return it. I overstepped the mark, I know that. I stepped over with large, unwieldy steps. And then I kept the truth from you, because I suppose… Oh, I think I thought it would all be over then. I wanted to keep you with me, selfishly."

"You are not selfish," Lavinia said, voice hushed. "You have never been selfish."

"I have been foolish, though."

She gave a short laugh, coming closer towards him. On impulse, he reached out his hand, and she put hers in it.

"I won't argue with you about that," she said, smiling. "And the answer, by the way, is yes."

His smile widened. "You will marry me? Penniless as I am?"

She gave a dramatic sigh and grinned up at him. "Somebody must, I suppose. And, unfortunately, I love you too, William Willenshire."

The carriage door opened again, and Lord Brennon came tumbling out.

"What on earth is..." he paused, seeing William standing there, hand in hand with Lavinia. His eyes bulged.

"Oh," he managed. "*Oh.*"

Epilogue

One Month Later

William stared down at the neat little envelope, his name written briskly across it in his father's handwriting.

All of his siblings had gotten a similar letter on their wedding days. He'd invited them all into his room, all of them in their wedding finery. There was a taut sort of silence hanging in the room.

"My letter was strangely comforting," Katherine said at last, breaking the silence. "He said that he always hoped I would marry Timothy. That shocked me, a little. That he could know me that well?"

Alexander huffed. "Well, he told *me* I was his greatest disappointment."

"I don't know what I'd rather hear," William muttered. "I don't know if I want to read it."

"Would you like me to read it for you?" Henry offered. "I could read it in my head, and aloud, if I think you'd like to hear it."

William bit his lip. "That's kind, Henry, but no. What I mean is... well, I don't know if I want to read it at all."

There was a silence after that. His siblings exchanged looks.

"You aren't him, Will," Katherine murmured, reaching across to put a hand on his shoulder. "Whatever you choose, we will support you."

He smiled weakly at his siblings. "I'm grateful to have you three, you know. I don't think I particularly understood just how grateful. I... I know I haven't always been the finest older brother, or the best Duke of Dunleigh, but..."

"Well, you certainly weren't the worst," Alexander put in, making the others laugh. William chuckled, shaking his head. He glanced down at the envelope again, and the smile faded from his face.

Picking up the envelope, he crossed the room to where a fire blazed in the hearth. He glanced over his shoulder at his siblings.

"Aren't any of you going to stop me?"

"It's your letter," Henry said firmly. "Your letter, your wedding day. You can do what you like, and we'll support you. We will."

He nodded, turning back to the flames. Letting the envelope dangle over the fire, he held his breath.

He let go.

The envelope landed in the edge of the grate, one corner beginning to smoulder and blacken, a single tongue of fire beginning to eat up the white paper.

William muffled a curse, darting down to snatch the letter out of the fire. It smoked, and he gave it a little shake, putting out any residual embers. When he dropped it back on the desk, only one corner had burned up. The contents, he guessed, would only be lightly blackened.

"Well," he said heavily. "That didn't work."

Alexander placed a hand on his shoulder. "You don't have to look at it now, you know. Why don't you enjoy your wedding day, and think about it afterwards?"

William smiled up at his brother, nodding slowly. "I think that's a good idea."

Outside, wedding bells began to peal.

**

Three Days Later

Lavinia picked up the envelope, lifting an eyebrow. "Is this it?"

William nodded. "There it is."

Their wedding day – and the next few days – had passed in a blur of wine, dancing, and laughter. William couldn't entirely believe that he *was* married, and to the most beautiful woman in the world.

At least, *he* thought that she was the most beautiful woman in the world.

Lavinia had kept her wedding-dress, a beautiful, lace-edged, ivory creation which suited her fiery hair and smooth, creamy skin. Her bouquet was mostly greenery, dappled with small white flowers, and matched William's button-hole posy. He'd pressed the posy between the pages of a book, to keep forever.

Today, she was wearing a simple muslin gown, probably one of her riding gowns. Lavinia had ridden Sapphire now too, and she and the horse seemed to be a perfect match.

William still did not love riding, but he was growing to like it more. Just a little more. Now that the horse which had killed his father was named, the creature seemed... well, more like an ordinary horse. Sometimes, the events of the past few months seemed like a hazy dream.

The families were settling down now. Katherine's pregnancy was common news, and they were all excited for the new baby. Their mother had set up a firm friendship with Lady Brennon, and the two women seemed remarkably good for each other. Miss Gillian was engaged to Lord Langley, who had apparently been ready to ride out to meet her at the country estate as soon as he knew she had left Bath and beg her to marry him. They seemed well suited.

It seemed odd, though, that the Willenshires were suddenly settled, with all the chaos behind them. Was this the end?

"If you want to destroy it," Lavinia said, cutting into his thoughts, "I won't stop you."

William let out a breath. "No. I want to read it. I should read it."

She smiled, and impulsively leaned down to kiss him.

"You're a brave man, Will. Go on, then. Let's see what your old man has to say."

William gave a burble of laughter at this. "You're a wretch. He'd have hated you."

"I certainly hope so."

He undid the envelope, pulling out a single sheet of good paper, covered in the old duke's handwriting. The corner of the page was singed. Lavinia met his eye and lifted her eyebrow questioningly.

"Don't ask," William mumbled, and began to read.

To My Eldest Son, William

My congratulations on your nuptials. As the dutiful son I know you are, you will have concluded your marriage before any of your brothers, I daresay. Katherine's role in this may be a little different, as you will now know.

I always saw myself in you when you were young, but as you grow older, I confess myself disappointed. You are a clever boy, dutiful, and will make a good duke, but I am not sure that I can see the fire and hardness in your spirit that a man ought to have. You are too sensitive, William, too soft.

But that is neither here nor there. You will be the next Duke of Dunleigh, and your wife will be a duchess. I hope you have chosen a rich woman, with excellent breeding. Do not worry about love or matters of the heart – they only complicate matters. I hope the future Duchess understands her role and place in the world and will not allow herself to be swayed by emotion or any sort of female weakness.

"Well," Lavinia said, allowing herself a small smile. "That is quite like me, don't you think? Emotionless, without any sort of *female weakness.*"

William chuckled. "As I said, my father would not have liked you. And it is a compliment, don't worry."

"I took it as such. Go on, keep reading."

The point is, you have done your duty, which is an excellent start. Now, to business. As you are my eldest son, I shall enclose some details which I will not add to your siblings' letters.

You have inherited your share of the fortune, but your work is not yet done.

William frowned, leaning forward. "What is that supposed to mean? Are there more terms? The lawyer never mentioned them."

Lavinia, hanging over his shoulder, nudged him. "Read on, read on."

I believe that a man should take charge of his own family, without interference. This interference includes friends, partners, and of course, family. I did not see fit to include my own family members in our circle, and certainly not those of your mother's. They would have gotten in the way, I think, of the way I chose to shape my family.

However, a gentleman cannot escape his duty, or the effects of any promises he may have been rash enough to make. Due to an old agreement, the details of which I shall not trouble you, I find myself with obligations towards a relative.

Your cousin, in point of fact, and her mother.

Now, at the time of your reading this letter, the matter may have been settled, but then again, it may not. The crux of the matter is that if this cousin is not married, it will be your obligation, William, to care for her and find her a suitable husband. I trust you will decide how involved she will become in your family.

Upon your wedding day and the receipt of this letter, a message will be sent to the woman, summoning her to the Willenshire estate, whereupon you may take charge of your duties.

That is all.
Your Devoted Father

There was a brief pause after William finished the letter. He read and reread the final part several times, not quite able to believe that the last words his father had ever directed to him on paper were simply *that is all*.

"A cousin? Which cousin?" Lavinia managed.

"Truly, I don't know. I don't believe we met any of our relatives. Father wouldn't allow it. We never even ran into any of them in London. I... I have no idea who he means. I must talk to the lawyer."

At that moment, there was a delicate tap on the door, and the butler stepped in, frowning.

"Forgive me, your Graces. I know you did not wish to be disturbed, but there is a rather singular occurrence. You... there are *visitors*."

He uttered the word with distaste. It was certainly improper to visit a pair of newlyweds on their honeymoon. William met Lavinia's eye.

"Oh? Visitors?"

"Yes. I told them to go, of course," the butler added, "but they were insistent. At last, I showed them into the *small* parlour. The thing is, your Grace..."

He hesitated, and William briefly shut his eyes. "Go on."

"The thing, the younger woman says that she is your cousin. The older one claims to be your aunt."

"Ah," William said. "Oh dear."

Lavinia managed a smile. "I think you'd better show them in, then, don't you?"

The End

Printed in Great Britain
by Amazon